SIREN SONG

GEORGE DISMUKES

This book is dedicated to my beloved Nadine, and to Kathy Pierce, dear friend & the world's best Beta Reader!

CHAPTER ONE

The Dream

S cott Carrington, thirty-seven years old, 6'2" with a thick shock of light brown hair and in great physical condition, descended slowly through crystal clear water. The only sounds were the air bubbles which he exhaled through his state of the art SCUBA air regulator. Indeed, all of his scuba equipment is the best that money can buy including his multi-colored blue BC-buoyancy compensator, his mask and especially his 'octopus,' the nick-name given to the air regulator and accompanying instruments which connect to his air supply. Scott has access to such luxurious equipment because he is a dive-master and assistant instructor at the Sport Divers of Houston Scuba Center just south of Houston. Scott is also a professional under-water photographer, and an extremely good one.

Something wasn't right about this dive because under normal circumstances, no diver would undertake a deep dive like this without a dive buddy. Scott looked around, did a 360-degree spin in the water, and confirmed that he was alone. A frightening prospect, even for a seasoned diver.

His descent was along a sheer vertical wall that seemed to plummet straight down forever. This wall was different from most walls found under-water because it was basically barren of plant and animal life. There should be corals and sea fans, and sea anemones, small crabs and cleaner shrimp, small colorful fish darting about. Instead, there was only a thin coat of greenish looking fern-like material. And at this depth, even the green color was fading and looking like a dull blue.

He checked the watch style depth gauge on his wrist and found that he was already at 100 feet beneath the surface, a depth nearing the onset of nitrogen narcosis, aka raptures of the deep. Divers also coin another phrase for the underwater inebriation. They call it, "Martini's Law."

Translated, that means, for each fifty feet of depth under water, the nitrogen narcosis factor equals drinking one martini on an empty stomach. A hundred feet down means a two martini zonk, etcetera. And it's great because when the diver returns to the surface, not only are they instantly sober again, but suffer no hangover. What could be better?

Scott carried with him an expensive, elaborate under-water camera. Sub-sea photography was not only his profession, but also his passion. He was always searching for that once in a lifetime photo. And on a few occasions, his quest had paid off. The results had been published in magazines devoted to diving. And Angie Harmon, his business partner / life partner had published more than one coffee table book of Scott's rare photographs. They sold very well in stores like Barnes & Noble, as well as on-line booksellers worldwide.

Suddenly, at about 120 feet, the 'wall' gave way to a huge cavern-like opening. It was a grotto, replete with mineral formations, stalactites and stalagmites measuring fifteen to twenty feet in length. They filled the grotto and gave it the appearance of being a giant maw, and an eerie looking maw at that, not unlike some sea creature's wide open mouth, ready to chomp down on a hapless victim.

Scientifically, the mineral formations were evidence that this entire cave-like structure had been above water at one time in history, perhaps millions of years ago. But now, Martini's Law gave the cavernous opening a frightening, ominous quality that sent chills up Scott Carrington's spine. Or was it only Martini's Law?

He halted his descent by gently moving his flippers back and forth a few times, then went horizontal and moved slowly, carefully forward into the opening. Progress was trepidatious, trying to negotiate through the huge mineral formations. Then Scott pulled up short. Something was there, in front of him, only a few feet away. But the light was dim, and he couldn't make it out. Whatever it was, his instincts said 'trouble' and he wanted to quickly back-pedal his way out of the grotto.

'Backing up' is difficult for a diver, and whatever it was started moving forward, toward him. He raised his camera, pointed in the general direction of the object and pressed the shutter button. An instant, bright flash went off, illuminating the creature that was closing in on him. It was grotesque. Uglier than anything he had ever seen.

And then, Scott Carrington awoke from his dream, screaming bloody murder. Angie Harmon, sleeping next to him, woke with a start.

"Same dream again?" she said, still groggy, and pushing up into a sitting position.

"Yeah," he said. "Same damn blasted dream. Exactly the same! Why? What's causing it? It's driving me batty."

Angie thought for a minute. "Maybe what's causing it isn't nearly as important as what to do about it to get it stopped."

Scott turned so he could look at her. "And what do you think that might be?"

"Don't ask me. It's not my dream. But if it was, I would want to face what I was seeing in the dream."

"What? Return to The Great Blue Hole? It's a practical certainty that I will. But what is that going to solve?"

"Well, for one thing, whatever 'it' is, is probably there waiting for you. Confront it. Kick it's ass, then we'll have an afternoon delight to celebrate!"

"That simple, huh?"

"No, I didn't say it would be simple. But from here, it seems necessary 'if' you ever plan on getting another good night's sleep."

Scott sat on the edge of the bed, looking at the wall, in the dark. "Why is it, you always have to be so frapping right?"

"I don't know," Angie said, as she snuggled back down in bed and pulled the covers up to her neck. "It's a curse!"

"A curse! Well, I know one thing, Missy. You'd better be glad you are so damn cute, or you would never get away with 'always being right'."

"Yeah? What would you do?"

"I don't know. You are cute. So, I don't have a plan for...whatever!"

"Um. Well, in that case, get back in this bed and cuddle up with me. I'm getting cold."

CHAPTER TWO

The Family Legend

It was a beautiful morning in the 7ᵗʰ grade orchestra class at Travis High School in Nassau Bay, Texas. The teacher had assigned a particularly pastoral selection of Celtic music for orchestra and harp. The harp solo was to sustain for several minutes. Something no-one objected to, because the harpist was a very talented, proficient young lady Named Meredith. Listening to Meredith play was the closest thing they had in orchestra class to perfection.

As Meredith began her solo, twelve-year-old James Harmon, seated not far from her in the string section, got a glassy stare in his eyes as he listened to the hypnotic music. After a minute or so, he set his cello aside, rose from his chair and walked to where Meredith was playing. He stood close to her, beside the harp, silently staring as he listened. That wasn't really so much a problem, but his close proximity to the girl as she played was unnerving her.

This did not go unnoticed by the orchestra teacher who left her podium and walked to where James was standing. She placed her hand on his left shoulder, but he made a sudden shrugging movement and brushed her hand away. Slightly shocked, the teacher put her hand on his shoulder again, and once again he brushed her hand away, this time turning toward her and barking, "Don't touch me!".

Having thus dismissed her, he returned his attention to Meredith. But James' radical behavior had frightened the poor girl and she had stopped playing.

"Continue," James demanded. And because she was afraid not to, Meredith resumed her recital on the harp, but she had a worried look on her face as she stared straight ahead, avoiding any eye contact with James.

The teacher tried a third time to gently take James by the shoulder and steer him back to his seat. But he quickly turned toward her and pushed her away, hard, screaming, "Don't touch me!" Again, he turned toward Mary Meredith and demanded, "Play! Don't stop!"

The teacher was now shocked at James Harmon's aberrant behavior. This was completely unlike him. She pressed a special button on the under-side of her desk that signaled for help. While she waited for school personnel to respond, she stayed away from James Harmon and let him enjoy Meredith's harp.

———

Al Harmon, James' father, a slightly stout man in his forties, but still in good shape, and good looking for his age with a shock of thick, sandy blond hair, sat in a comfortable chair across the desk from Ms. Margaret Stone, the school principal. Ms. Stone had a file open in front of him on his deck and paged through several documents.

James sat in a wooden chair in the outer office, next to

the secretary's desk. He slouched and was looking at the floor, clearly dejected and unhappy. There were glass panels separating this ante-office and Ms. Stone's inner office. James could have viewed the meeting between his father and the principle if he had wanted to. But he kept his gaze on the floor in front of him. From here, the only sound was the secretary typing on the computer keyboard.

"I don't know what to think of all this," Ms. Stone was saying to Al Harmon. "James is one of our highest achievers. I mean, his grades are probably the best in the school, and this is his freshman year. He obviously has a high IQ, and I'll tell you, many times, children with high IQs are somewhat lax. Einstein was a school dropout, for instance. But that isn't the case with James. He's a model student. He shows tremendous ambition. He's prompt, never plays hooky. Always has his homework done on time. He's always been very polite to his teachers, always pleasant, upbeat." Ms. Stone waves his her at the school records.

Al Harmon sits quietly, watching Ms. Stone, listening to the woman speak. The fingers of both hands are interlocked. His knees are crossed.

"Something is obviously bothering him. Tell me, do you own a boat? What I mean to ask is, does your family have anything to do with maritime? Do you own a boat, or anything like that? Something to do with water?"

"Sure," Al Harmon replies. "I'm in the maritime shipping business. Petroleum, mainly. I own a few tankers. Or more accurately, me and the *bank,* own some tankers. Why? What does that have to do with anything?"

The school principal pulled several sheets of large drawing paper from James' folder and hands them to Al Harmon. Al studied them for a couple of minutes.

"James did these?"

"Yes, he did."

The drawings are very good, but also slightly mysterious. Every one of them is about the same subject; an under-water depiction of a beautiful woman. Beautiful, yes. Yet somehow evil.

"My God!" Al Harmon gasped.

"What's the matter?" Ms. Stone asked.

"Um, I'm not sure. Maybe nothing. It's just, well, an old family tradition. Wait, tradition isn't the right word. 'Legend.' Yeah, legend is the right word. I had no idea James was aware of it, but it has to be what influenced these."

Al separates a couple of the drawing from the others and hands them back across the desk to the principal.

Ms. Stone studies the drawings. "Who's the girl?"

"Like I said, a family legend, passed down through old family records. I don't think it means anything. But I've always kind of wondered. One can never be blind to the possibility of some wild...over the top, freaking...! You know, there's lots of, let's call it 'fantasy' that comes from old sailors. I guess there wasn't much to do at night, sitting around, drinking grog, aboard an old three master ship at sea. They sat around and drank and entertained one another with light-hearted bullsh—I mean, lore, fantasy, 'sea tales'. They made stuff up. Sea monsters, mermaids. Sirens. Later on, those tales began to be told on television and everyone accepted them as forgivable fiction, especially horse operas, you know, westerns."

"Yes, yes," Ms. Stone said, watching the body language of Al Harmon closely. "Tell me about the girl, Mr. Harmon."

"The girl, yes. Well, she's not really a girl... or woman. She's a siren."

"What?"

Al Harmon, clearly nervous, rises from his chair and walks to the window where he looks out and stares at an empty playground. Then, he repeats his last sentence while still looking out the window.

"She's a siren."

"Siren?"

Al Harmon turns back to face the principle. "Yeah, a siren. You know? Like in Greek Mythology. According to our family history, James' ancestor, his great–great grandfather was the victim of a...siren. I mean, it can't be taken seriously, of course. It's fun to banter around at the Christmas party punch bowl, but I'm a little surprised to see it surface like this." Al Harmon waved his hand at the drawings, then shakes his head. "I hope that isn't what's bothering James. I, I'm sure it can't be."

"Then what would be the reason for her repeated appearance in these drawings? And she looks almost identical in all of them. That alone tells something." Margaret Stone looked from the drawings, to Al Harmon.

"It's anybody's guess? Look, James is twelve years old. Who knows what kind of horse shit goes on in a twelve-year old's head? Certainly not a silly fable about sea sirens. Would it?"

"Or perhaps, siren feathers!" the principal said with a chuckle.

"What?"

"Oh, I'm sorry. I was sort of an aficionado of Greek Mythology in my college days. Weren't the sirens supposed to be half bird, half woman? The reason for the 'feathers' quip."

It was at this moment that Al Harmon's response let the cat out of the bag. "The original three were, yes."

"Original three? You mean there were more? In legend of course?"

Al Harmon's demeanor becomes very matter-of-fact. "Yes, well, 'according to 'legend' they eventually mated with sea creatures, and, sometimes with men, humans. The sirens weren't exactly what you would call, 'models of moral virtue'! More like examples of moral turpitude. Anyway, 'according to legend,' when they grew tired of their chosen mates, they would lure them beneath the waves, then suck their breath away with a deceptive kiss... and after that, devour part of the body."

Margaret Stone made a face. "Ugh! Talk about a black widow! Is that supposedly what happened to James' great–great?"

"Grandfather? Yeah, 'supposedly'. His body was never recovered. A shark probably got what was left of it by the time the siren got through with him. I mean, what difference does it make? What we're dealing with here is bullshit, a tall tale. A family fable. What I think is. The great-great screwed up and lost his ship due to some kind of carelessness. Maybe he was admired by his men, so they came up with a barrel full of crap to cover up what really happened."

"Keep trying and you might convince yourself of that," Margaret Stone said.

Al Harmon turned and stared at Margaret Stone for a long moment. Then, a confession. "I'm not sure what I'm up against here, much less what to do about it."

"Isn't your son a scuba diver?"

"Just about to graduate scuba school," Al Harmon says with obvious pride. "So far as we know, the youngest diver in the U.S. Hot damn, I'm proud of the boy!" Al Harmon smiled broadly.

"Then, if I may suggest, take him diving."

"What? Oh, well, I intend to. We're going to Belize, to dive The Great Blue Hole."

"The Great Blue Hole? I've heard of that place. Isn't that kind of a dangerous dive for a beginner?"

"Nah. James is very skilled. And besides, he be surrounded like Custer at the Little Big Horn with dive masters, assistant dive masters, me!"

"Well, good then. Let him face his 'siren'. If she's not there, at least it will give him the chance to get her out of his system."

Al Harmon turned and once again looked out the window. "And what if she *is* there, Ms. Stone? What if she is there?"

CHAPTER THREE

Graduation

7:00 p.m. The location is the Sport Divers of Houston Scuba Center, located on Hwy 45 South near Webster, Texas. The store is well stocked with the latest scuba diving equipment, all of which is beautifully displayed throughout the store. Everything from scuba tanks to regulators and ancillary equipment such as depth gauges to attach to first stage regulators when building an octopus. The store has a nice smell of 'new' about it, and a comfortable feeling that assures customers who visit here of the knowledge and professionalism of the store's operators. One of the most attractive displays are the brightly colorful BCs (Buoyancy Compensators), which are displayed adjacent to the wet suits, equally colorful. In fact, so colorful that some customers in the store joke about them.

Now tell me, just how much sense does it make to go in the water dressed up like a big fishing lure?"

The classroom, in the back of the store is filled to capacity on this particular evening because this is a graduating class. Not only are registered students present, but family members of those students, all there to cheer on their special loved one and all armed with cameras or cell phones with cameras to record the moment their special person receive their hard earned 'C' card.

As each name is called, the student diver comes forward and is handed their bright blue NAUI 'C' card. Then they pose for a graduation picture with their instructor. In this case, there are two instructors—Ken Malloy and Scott Carrington. Each one flanks the student and smiles for the camera. They both shake hands with each student and tell them 'congratulations'.

Twelve-year-old James Harmon, however, is a little bit disappointed. Because he isn't yet fifteen years of age, he receives a different kind of 'C' card, a simple white, cardboard version. It doesn't even have his photo I.D. on it. There is no glamour whatsoever to the cardboard card, no pop, no glitz. It isn't fair and James is slightly pissed.

Ken Malloy shakes James' hand as he hands him the card, sandwiches James between himself and Scott Carrington and all three pose for a photo being taken by Al Harmon.

Ken says in an effort to comfort James, "I know that you worked just as hard as everyone else for your certification. In fact, your scores on the written test were better than most. Sorry about the wimpy, cardboard card, *but* it will automatically roll over and you will get a blue plastic one on your fifteenth birthday, with a photo I.D. and the whole enchilada."

"Yeah, I know. But that rule sucks anyway," James says with a dour look on his face.

"You're right, James. It does," Ken said.

After everyone had received their card and settled down a little, a presentation began, hosted by Scott Carrington.

"As you all know," Scott began, "one way that scuba shops stay alive is by offering dive trips to exotic locations. The usual graduation trip is to Cozumel, off the east coast of Mexico. They have some beautiful reefs there, clear water and some shallows where beginner divers can do their check out dives, which, by the way, is where we are really supposed to hold graduation. But we have discovered that some people's work schedules preclude them being able to make a trip right away. So, that's why we have modified the standard rule to having graduation a little prematurely. With that said, I'm here to offer a different kind of trip, and not generally one for beginner divers.

"We have a dive safari going to The Great Blue Hole of the Caribbean. This is a very exotic trip. We only go to the Great Blue Hole about once a year because quite honestly, the Great Blue Hole isn't everybody's idea of a good time. It's a very deep dive, a little dangerous and more than a little spooky. Besides, there aren't that many charters that go there due to the distance involved, and…well."

A bright picture came up on the big screen TV located against the wall at one end of the room. The photo was an aerial view of The Great Blue Hole and the surrounding coral formations.

"This is The Great Blue Hole of The Caribbean," Scott narrated. "It is over one thousand feet across and four hundred and eight feet deep. Millions of years ago, it was a cavern, complete with a dome-like ceiling. But following the last ice age, about fifty thousand years ago, the water level began to rise. The Great Blue Hole was swallowed by the sea. In fact, the entire island where The Hole is located was swallowed up. The ceiling over the cavern became inundated with water, weakened and collapsed; caved in, exposing the cavern to the world of daylight. Almost! As you know, water filters light, so the farther you descend, the less light there is. And colors are filtered out too. When you go past sixty or seventy feet, everything looks blue. Even if you're wearing a bright yellow BC, it looks blue."

Several more colorful photos are flashed up on the TV screen showing various kinds of coral and sea life that exists on Lighthouse Reef and in particular the area immediately surrounding The Great Blue Hole. These were intricate, underwater photographs taken by Scott Carrington himself on a previous trip to The Hole. A beautiful photo of a spiny lobster popped up on the screen. Scott told a humorous story.

"On this particular trip, a guy named Oscar Buck said he was going to go out and catch enough spiny lobsters for everyone to enjoy for supper. We all said yeah, yeah. But then, much to our surprise, Oscar Buck did just that. He came back in fairly short order with eight beautiful, spiny lobsters. Well, we cooked 'em up, served 'em up, and then somebody said we needed butter for them. Everyone agreed. Someone grabbed a bottle out of the pantry that was supposedly butter in a squeeze bottle. We passed it around, everyone squeezed butter on their lobster, and then got down to business. Well, it turned out, the butter was not butter. It was dish soap. Everybody's lobster was ruined, and we wound up eating beans, with lobster on the table!"

There was a lot of relaxed laughter. Then Scott went to the next picture. Everybody stopped laughing. It was a close-up photo of a large hammerhead shark, swimming straight toward the camera.

"This is the one of the drawbacks to diving The Great Blue Hole," Scott said. There are several of these characters who live there, and nobody can figure out why. Sharks are like swimming garbage cans. They eat anything and everything, but mostly, they eat a lot. There just isn't that much for a large shark to eat in The Hole. Essentially, it's barren of life."

He put another picture on the screen. This picture was not pretty. It was in half light, and ominous looking. It was a picture of a cavernous opening in the side of a wall containing mineral formations.

"These are grottos in the wall of The Great Blue Hole. They begin at about 120 feet from the surface. That's the ceiling, and the floor of the grottos levels off at about 150 or 155 feet. These grottos extend around the entire circumference of the hole and marine scientists suspect they are part of an underwater, and underground network of caves which honeycomb all of Lighthouse Reef, where The Great Blue Hole is located, plus possibly the entire country of Belize which in any case sits on a giant plate of ancient limestone."

Scott hits the remote button and displays several more pictures of various sea life in and around The Hole.

"Overall," Scott Carrington continues, "The Great Blue Hole is a very different kind of dive. It certainly isn't for everybody because if you go there, you won't see the myriad of colorful fish like you do on a regular reef dive, say like, Palancar Reef at Cozumel. There isn't an array of coral. Actually, inside the Hole itself, there isn't any coral at all. It is an undersea anomaly. And the main reason for going there is just because it is a deep dive. Once you have dived the Great Blue Hole, most people feel, and almost everyone agrees, you are in a different category from that time forward. You are a deep diver, someone to be taken seriously. You may, if you wish, wear the special 'one hundred feet' designation necklace made of black coral." Scott indicated the black coral necklace he is wearing.

"Anyway, on assent, you will have to make at least one decompression dive to make sure you don't get the bends. And believe me, you *do not want* the bends. As discussed in your class, the bends cripple. The bends kill. And at the very least, the bends are one of the most painful things you would ever have the misfortune to experience *in your life*! I've only seen one person with the bends, and it scared the living hell out of me. It was an older guy. He should have cut five minutes off of his standard bottom time, but he was having a good time and didn't do that. When he came up, everything seemed fine. We pulled up on the beach to have lunch. He was sitting there, eating. Suddenly a pain hit him. Not too bad at first, but it didn't go away. Instead, it kept getting more severe. By that night, he as in the hospital and stayed there for two weeks. To this very day, he cannot use the fingers in his left hand.

"So, knowing all of this, the question begs, why dive The Great Blue Hole? Well, I guess it's the same answer that applies to a mountain climber going up the Matterhorn; *'because it is there.'* Besides, it's fun to stand around at parties with a glass in your hand and casually remark, offhandedly of course, 'Aw sure, I've dived The Great Blue Hole!'"

And at this, everybody laughed.

Later, after the presentation was over and student graduates were milling around the store looking at diver's equipment they would like to have, James Harmon, accompanied by his father, approached Ken Malloy.

"Great presentation, Mr. Malloy. I think you managed to scare the crap out of a few people."

"I confess, I did it on purpose. The absolute worst thing a diver can do is get too relaxed out there. Every sentence should begin and end with the word, 'safety.' 'Stay alive, cut five'! That's my motto."

James nods in agreement, but then changes subjects. "Did my bang-stick come in?" James asks.

"Yeah, it did," Ken said, as he stepped behind a counter to retrieve the piece of equipment. "But like I told you, technically this is your father's bang stick. I can't sell this thing to anyone under the age of twenty-one."

"Yeah, I know," James said as he accepted the strange looking, six-foot-long rod from Ken.

"I can't stress enough just how dangerous this weapon is. Somebody could get injured or killed, very easily. I mean, it's a firearm, just with a modified long barrel."

"Listen to what the man is telling you," Al Harmon said to his son. James nods. "I don't know why you feel like you have to have that thing anyway," Al says.

"Sharks, Dad. Sharks. Didn't you see Jaws?"

"Yeah, but that shark was made out of plastic! A bang stick wouldn't have done much good."

James eyes his father, then turns back to Ken Malloy.

Ken reached behind the counter one more time and withdrew a blue box, three by six inches. "Okay, here's the waterproof ammo. These are .357-gauge bullets. Fit one round of ammo into the head, screw the sleeve on, and it's ready. At least this model has a safety catch. Most don't even have that. But remember, it only takes five pounds of pressure to release the trigger mechanism. I recommend test firing it without a live round, and above water, before you actually go in the water with it. Get a feel for how much pressure it takes to release the trigger. I'm a little nervous selling you this thing. And I have to hand the ammunition directly to your father," Ken says, as he hands the box to Al Harmon. "The law says I cannot place it in your possession."

"I understand. Don't worry, I get the point. I'll be careful. I'll be *very* careful," James says. "It's just that I've heard about those hammerheads in The Great Blue Hole, and everything I have read about hammerheads says they are unpredictable, *and* a little bit nasty tempered. I don't intend to wind up being a filet of diver sandwich."

The trio chuckled at that. "Okay," Ken said. "I just hope I don't wind up regretting selling this thing to you."

Armed with his bang stick, James is happy, despite the cardboard 'C' as he and his father exit the front door of the dive shop.

CHAPTER FOUR

Mysterious Maris

San Leon, Texas is a small hamlet on the Texas coast, population, 5,000, assuming you count a few dogs. It is located approximately half-way between Houston and Galveston. Despite being sandwiched between two metroplexes, San Leon is an independent world of its own. The population is small, many of the San Leon-ites know one another, and the local motto is: "San Leon, a small drinking community with a large fishing problem."

In fact, San Leon is situated on a small peninsula. Almost tiny when you look at it on a satellite map and shaped roughly like a cat's claw on one side, which hangs off into Dickinson Bay, which is an adjunct to Galveston Bay. People in San Leon are very defensive about their micro-community and take great pride in being San Leon-ites. Rightfully so.

A few defining features of the peninsula are that it holds the prestigious distinction of being home base to not one, but two of the nation's largest oyster titans to be found anywhere in the United States, and a brewery that makes some of the best rum to be found anywhere. An opinion which is bolstered frequently by connoisseurs of rum. Even the "El Numero Uno" rum of Puerto Rico is challenged by the rum of San Leon which features a parrot on the label. Some would even say the famous Puerto Rican rum is put to shame.

It is also home to some of the best seafood restaurants to be found anywhere along the coast. One case in point is The Pier Six Seafood Restaurant, located on the north-east side of the peninsula. The restaurant features an upper-class atmosphere which is justified because the kitchen is under the control of a world class chef, and the food is so renowned that people drive the thirty or so miles from Houston just to eat at The Pier Six.

Outdoor tables strategically situated on a wooden decked veranda are a feature of the Pier Six. The veranda hangs over the water, adjacent to the Pier Six Marina, a water dock shared by yachts which berth alongside fishing vessels. The overall atmosphere is not 'made up' as in some trendy locations. There is nothing phony at The Pier Six Restaurant, it is absolutely real. The very atmosphere is real, 100% genuine. And that fact adds to the enjoyment of the succulent seafood.

On this beautiful June night, one of those outdoor tables on the veranda played host to a party of several people celebrating the certification of twelve-year-old James Harmon, son of Al Harmon. James was proud of himself, having just received his SCUBA certification. So was his father, sitting beside him, relaxing and having fun. But this party had a double purpose. It was also a bon voyage party for the group of people gathered at the table. People about to embark on a sea safari to The Great Blue Hole of The Caribbean.

Seated at the table with James and his father, were the scuba instructor, Divemaster Ken Malloy, photographer and assistant Dive Master, Scott Carrington, plus Scott's girlfriend and business partner, Angie Holland. One other person was there, Captain Gordon Hughes, owner and Captain of Siren Song. One more person was supposed to be there, deckhand, D J. But in typical form, D J was late.

Angie was a stunningly beautiful woman, 5'6', very well built, hazel eyes, dark brunette hair that hung just past her shoulders. But her beauty was somehow obscured, second in place to her pursuit of money. And so, her eyes had the look of always sizing somebody up, as though she was always hunting for her next client. There was very little 'just for fun' about Angie. That is, not until now… maybe.

The other person there; Captain Gordon Hughes, devoted owner of the eighty-foot yacht affectionately named Siren Song, was relaxed more than usual and having a good time. He and Al Harmon had hit it off, perhaps they had so much in common. Gordon Hughes had a yacht. Al Harmon owned tanker ships. But they were both careers dependent on the sea, and thus, both men shared similar problems. Vastly different in some ways, but amazingly the same in others. At the moment, they were discussing maritime laws and required permits to do just about anything. Their shared commiserating made the beer taste better.

Siren Song rests comfortably, moored in her berth only yards away from where the celebration is taking place. Siren Song is an exceptionally beautiful yacht, even when compared with other yachts. She has a commanding look to her, as if she is ready for any adventure, with a guarantee to deliver her passengers to any destination, comfortably, and safely.

Gordon Hughes is proud of his yacht and proud of the service he offers. Gordon has the look of a modern-day sea captain. He is deeply sun tanned, has piercing blue eyes and a brown shock of hair that always seems to be 'almost' combed, but not quite. Gordon is in his mid-fifties, stout, broad in the shoulders and is somebody you didn't mess with. He is very dedicated to his profession, and his profession is the enjoyment and comfort of people who entrust their aqua safaris to him.

To that end, the interior of Captain Gordon's Siren Song is appointed in the epitome of elegance. Everything about her exterior and inside her bespeaks it.. The furniture in the large salon reflects expensive opulence. The sofa and matching chairs are expensive overstuffed leather with electric reclining sections. The end tables and the gorgeous, slightly oversized dark-wood coffee table bespeak elegance and is sans adornment save for several spread-out editions of THE SALTWATER ANGLER MAGAZINE, the premier fishing magazine for serious sportsmen and women anywhere along the Texas/Louisiana coast. There is one other conspicuous item on the coffee table. It is a coffee table book by Scott Carrington entitled. *Beneath the Waves*, featuring the spectacular photography of the very talented man.

Siren Song instrument console has only the best, most expensive navigation equipment that money can buy. Below deck, six roomy state rooms feature large beds with the best hand-made mattresses. The rest rooms are equipped with brass fixtures and glowing, well-lit mirrors.

But Siren Song is a yacht specifically and exclusively

outfitted for scuba diving. The stern of the boat removes any doubt. It is equipped with special racks to hold aluminum 80 scuba tanks. And there is a special air pump installed there to recharge scuba tanks which have been depleted of air from a dive.

Additionally, this is not a yacht that entertains standard 'day diving' to nearby reefs or in the case of The Gulf of Mexico, trips to the Flower Gardens or to tie up alongside oil rigs to spear grouper.

Siren Song is a specialty yacht catering to well healed people who desire a different kind of dive safari. Siren Song specializes in charters that feature targets not so much in the Gulf of Mexico, if ever. But rather, Caribbean dive trips to places like Belize, The Bay of Honduras, Hispañola, and many other Caribbean Islands.

To Al Harmon, it seems like the perfect way to celebrate James Harmon's maiden dive trip; a safari aboard Siren Song, to one of the most exotic dive spots in the world, The Great Blue Hole of the Caribbean.

According to NAUI, the National Association of Underwater Instructors, the youngest anybody can be certified is at fifteen years of age, but not everybody is the son of a shipping magnate.

Al Harmon is owner and CEO of the Sargasso Tanker Lines, and his influence has a long reach. So it was that James Harmon was allowed to take scuba instruction from the top dive master to be found anywhere in Texas, and be certified as a "Junior Diver," a certification that will automatically roll over to a regular 'C' card when James turned fifteen.

James was now a junior diver and this party was to celebrate that fact. Everybody at the large table were eating, talking, laughing, kibitzing, having fun. A waiter arrived with a special cake that had been prepared to present to James. On the cake, the letters S-C-U-B-A were completed to spell out, "Some Come Up Barely Alive."

Everybody laughed at this including James, who commented, "That isn't what SCUBA stands for!"

Everyone laughed again. Then Al Harmon said, "You'll have to forgive this young man. He just graduated from SCUBA class and he hasn't gotten his sense of humor back yet."

"So, just how good a student was James?" Angie Holland asked. Her one admitted weakness, besides Scott, in her otherwise brass exterior, is kids. She doesn't have any, but she loves them and wishes desperately that she did have at least one.

"One of the best," Ken said. "Matter of fact, he slaughtered just about everybody in his class on the written quiz."

"Really?" Angie teased. "Okay, let's check it out. James, what is the one-twenty rule?"

"One hundred-and-twenty minutes bottom time is how many minutes a diver has at the beginning of a dive, starting on the surface. But for every foot the diver goes down, that number has to be deducted from the 120. For example, if the diver descends to eighty feet, they only have 40 minutes bottom time, which starts at the surface. And by that I mean, 'bottom time' begins the moment a diver leaves the surface. So, if it takes five minutes to get down to eighty feet, in reality, they only have thirty-five minutes to look around before they have to start back up. The good news is bottom time ends the minute they leave eighty feet and start back up."

Everybody at the table applauded James's correct response. "Wow! He's really got it down," Angie said as she clapped.

"Wait, there's more!" James says as he holds up his hands. Even though, according to the J card, the diver might have thirty-five minutes bottom time, my instructor," James indicates Ken Malloy at the table, "strongly suggests that you 'cut five'; meaning although presumably you have thirty-five minutes on the bottom, abandon ship at thirty minutes. Take no chances on the bends. You also give yourself a little extra time in case you encounter any problems."

"Wow! Very good! *Very* good!" Scott Carrington says as he applauds. "So, let's quit messing around and cut that cake. It looks delicious. I want that big 'S' over on the left side!"

"Ung uh!" James says. "That's mine!"

The Pier Six waiter did the honors of cutting the cake and passing it around. As people taste their piece of cake, the conversation takes a turn.

Scott commented to Gordon Hughes, "SIREN SONG is an interesting name for a yacht. How did you come up with that?"

Captain Hughes looked toward the fantail of his yacht, only yards away. "A couple of reasons," he said. "When I was a kid, my dad had two boats named Siren. The first one was a twenty-three-foot Chris Craft wooden hull cabin cruiser which he called 'The Siren.' A good boat to be sure. But it didn't take long for him to decide that boat was just not big enough. After that, he had a thirty-two-footer, also a Chris Craft wooden hull *twin screw* cabin cruiser that he called the Siren II."

"So, family tradition," Angie said.

"Yeah, family tradition," Captain Hughes affirmed as he nodded his head.

"How do you think your dad came up with the idea of 'Siren' to begin with? Ken Malloy asked.

"Not sure. The call of the sea, that kind of thing. I never knew a man that liked to fish as much as he did. We were on that boat every weekend, without fail, headed for one reef or another. I got conscripted to be the deck hand. I don't remember ever getting to vote on that. But it wasn't so bad." Something about his words sounded hollow, unfinished.

"Why do I get the feeling there's more to it than that?" Ken pressed.

Captain Hughes' mood became a little more somber. He got a faraway look in his eye. Ken immediately saw this. "So! It would appear there is more, n'est ce pas?"

Captain Hughes was silent for several moments. He took a deep drink of his beer, then began to tell a story. "When I was a kid in Corpus Christ, there was a drive-in theater on Port Avenue called *'The Buccaneer.'* I'll never forget it, because there was a huge mural painting on the back side of the theater screen. It was a scene of a beautiful mermaid sitting on a rock in the middle of Corpus Christi Bay. She was drinking from a pink conch shell. I was always captivated by that painting. Hot damn, it was beautiful! Then, when I was barely a teenager, we were making an early morning run out to a reef that my dad liked where there were always lots of trout. I was sitting alone on the bow of the boat, just feeling the wind against me. It's kind of quiet there, you know. There's a special feeling. Anyway, I was looking around, enjoying the way the early morning sun was glistening across the water. Then, just for a split second, I thought, 'just for a split second,' understand, that I saw that very same scene with the mermaid, but in real life."

"You mean you saw an actual mermaid?" James Harmon asked.

"Ah... It was so quick. Just a momentary glance. A mirage. I'm sure it wasn't real, but I've gotta tell you, it was goose-bump time."

"Wow! That's a neat story," James said. "So, do you believe in Sirens... or mermaids?"

"That's a difficult question," Captain Gordon Hughes said with a half-smile.

Angie eyed the Captain. "Doesn't seem like the question is so difficult. It's the answer, perhaps, that is difficult. Eh, Captain?"

"There's a lot of fables about the sea," Gordon says, starting to sound a little defensive. "Old sailors must not have had much to do on those long nights aboard wind powered ships except to sit around and dream up bullshit. The problem came to be that a lot of that bullshit wound up in books. That gave the bullshit credibility which it didn't deserve long ago, doesn't deserve today. Whatever."

"Perhaps. But what James asked about is *you*. Specifically, *you*! Do *you* believe in mermaids, sirens, whatever?" Angie was having fun, pressing the captain and watching him begin to squirm. This kind of thing was her specialty, one of her finest talents.

"Not sure," Captain Hughes said in a slightly louder voice, now a little more defensively. "The jury is still out."

"Jury? What jury? It was just a conversational question. You know, having fun."

"Look, the answer is, I don't know. I admit, I've experienced a couple of strange things out there during my lifetime. You know, you know... You know, well, the ancient Greeks, and they weren't the only ones, had all kinds of tales about sirens and mermaids. Some people say it was just myth. But what was the true origin of myth? Seems like there had to be some basis in fact for it somewhere along the line. What was the reason for any of it? Where did it start? We just don't know. You know? Let's talk about something else. How's that cake, James?"

"Good!" James said as he took another bite. 'Some Come Up Barely Alive'. I like that. It's a good one!"

Several people at the table looked at one another and wondered at Captain Hughes' strange reaction. After all, it was just dinner conversation. But the subject had unexpectedly rattled the captain.

Angie decided to change the subject, and justifiably so. "Well I think it's time we talked about the trip. Is everyone geared up and ready for the big dive safari to The Great Blue Hole?"

Indeed, that was the 'other' reason for this gathering; a bon voyage party. Everyone at this table would be aboard Siren Song in one capacity or another for a long trip across the Gulf and into the Caribbean to a place located off the coast of Belize known as The Great Blue Hole.

"The Hole" was located inside Lighthouse Reef, a twenty-two-mile-long reef located seventy-five miles off the coast of Belize. The Hole was an ancient cave, now underwater, a thousand feet across and four hundred plus feet deep. At some point in antiquity, the roof had caved in, exposing The Hole to daylight, although 'daylight' was now below water. It was a popular dive spot for those with the financial means and imagination to get there. Captain Hughes was one of the few charter captains anywhere to organize dive parties for the long trip.

Why not station his boat in Belize and fly people in there who wanted to go to The Great Blue Hole? Because, "Getting there is half the fun!" Siren Song was outfitted specifically for divers, up to and including a compressor for refilling scuba tanks. Such equipment would only be needed for long distance trips such as this one.

However, with all of that said, this would be the last long distance trip for Captain Hughes or Siren Song, because berthing her at Placencia, on the Belize mainland is precisely what the captain had planned for his yacht. So, this would be a bon voyage party in more ways than one.

The table chatter turned to all the things people wanted to do on their trip. They were so involved with the happy making that nobody noticed a small wake in the marina which revealed something was swimming just below the surface, very close to where their table was situated.

Suddenly, James Harmon grabbed at his forehead and wobbled, as if starting to swoon. He quickly clutched the edge of the table to steady himself, but he was still weaving slightly. His father was the first to respond. He stood up and grabbed James arm to help steady him. "What's the matter, Son?"

"I don't know. I just had... it was like a dream. A, a vision. I saw this white sand beach that curved around an incredibly beautiful quiet lagoon. Small waves, beautiful, swaying palm trees. The air smelled clean and sweet, like it was perfumed with flowers. There were birds. Not seagulls. These birds were dark colored and had scissor tails."

"Frigate birds?"

"I don't know. Maybe. I guess."

"You saw all of that in just a moment?" James' father looked at him closely.

"Yeah. Like I said, it was like a vision of some kind."

"And you're the only one here who hasn't been drinking!"

Everyone laughed.

James sat down in his seat and took a large bite of cake. "Maybe it was a sugar high. Let me try again!"

Everybody laughed again.

Al Harmon sat down. But he mused about James' vision. James had never been to the Caribbean. He had never seen a frigate bird in his whole life. If he had never seen a frigate bird, how could he 'envision' one?

The party progressed on track, but minutes later, a small, exotic looking woman, with beautiful, long hair, dressed in a light blue full-length evening dress, approached the table where the party of revelers were laughing and chatting with each other.

As she approached the table, the woman smiled and interrupted their conversation by saying, "Excuse me. Is one of you Captain Gordon Hughes?"

"I am," Captain Hughes replied.

The petite woman turned her slightly almond shaped eyes toward the captain as she extended her hand in greeting. "Hi. I'm sorry to interrupt your dinner, but I have been told that you are about to shove off for Belize. To, The Great Blue Hole, I believe?"

"Yes. That's right."

"Do you have room for one more passenger?"

"Well, I don't know. We might," the captain said. "This is a dive trip. Are you a certified diver?"

"One of the best," the woman said with a smile. "My

name is Maris." She extended her hand to shake hands with Gordon. "What time do you weigh anchor?"

"Tomorrow morning, eight o-clock."

"Great. I'll see you then."

"Well, wait a minute! Ken Malloy said. "I'm the dive master on this trip and I haven't agreed to..."

The exotic looking Maris gave Ken Malloy a quick glance, turned and was gone as quickly as she had appeared.

"What the hell was that?" Ken Malloy suddenly said. "She can't just jump on board like that. She needs to be screened. You didn't get a chance to ask to see her 'C' card or anything. Where's her money? Shit! I think we just got boogered."

"I know. That was weird. It was so quick that I didn't have a chance to ask for her 'C' card, or anything else for that matter. No matter. We'll check her out in the morning, real good. If she doesn't pass muster, she damn sure won't get on board."

"Well, I hear you. But I'm not going to put up with this. Something about her just didn't sit right. And I want to be paid in full before Miss Almond Eyes sets one foot aboard the boat."

Everyone else at the table has fallen silent, listening to the exchange between Ken Malloy and Gordon Hughes.

Suddenly, a middle-aged man, half in the bag, sitting at a near-by table turned to Gordon and asked, "Excuse me. I hate to be nosy, but who was that beautiful blond woman that were just talking to? I'm asking only because she looks very familiar."

"Blond?" Gordon said. "Blond? She was a brunette, right?" He turned to Ken Malloy.

Ken looked a little confused. "Yeah, brunette, for sure."

The man at the next table stared at the two men for a minute. Then said, "Jesus! I must be more swacked than I thought. She looked blond to me. But hell, what do I know?"

James shook his head in agreement. "He's right. She was blond haired."

Ken turned to Angie. "Blond," Angie said.

"Brunette," Scott Carrington said.

"Too weird!" James said. "What was she, Dad?"

Al Harmon blinked. "Well now I'm not sure. I thought she as a brunette, but now, I just don't know."

"You probably weren't looking at her hair!" Angie said, humorously accusing. Everyone chuckled at this and the subject turned to other things. But Ken Malloy had a concerned look on his face. Something wasn't sitting right with him, and the safety of everyone on board was his responsibility, especially when they went in the water with scuba gear on.

"You know what," Ken says. "I'm not waiting until in the morning. I'm going after her right now and find out a little more about her *right now*. I'm not waiting till in the morning." With that, Ken Malloy rises from the table and heads in the direction the mysterious Maris retreated. In so doing he passes D J, Captain Gordon's deck hand, who is arriving late to the party. "Hey, D J!"

"Hey, Dude! Where ya going?"

"I'm chasing that woman that just left."

"Sounds like a plan," D J says, as he makes his way casually through the restaurant to the door leading outside to the veranda. He waves as he approaches the table.

"Sorry I'm late. So, who was the beautiful broad I just passed? She looked like she was leaving from our table."

"She's your type, is she?" Angie said a little sarcastically.

"Well, she might be if she wasn't so much older than me." D J found a seat and plopped down.

"Older than you?" Angie said. "I don't think she's any older than you. How old are you, D J?"

"Twenty-two glorious years old. Everything works and I'm feeling good. Looking good too, from what the chicks tell me. Take out to make out!"

"Enjoy it while you can, you damn pup," Gordon says, a little enviously.

"Twenty-two?" Angie says. "She might even be younger than you."

"Are we talking about the same person? That short broad with the long blond hair in the evening dress?"

"Brunette," Scott said.

"Oh. Then we must be talking about two different people. Because the one I saw was definitely a blond, around thirty-five. Big gazoombas!" D J indicated breasts with his hands.

"No wonder you didn't see the right color of her hair," Angie said. Everyone at the table laughed.

"So, where's Ken going?" D J asked.

"He went to look for the broad... woman."

"Oh, yeah. Now I remember. If he finds her, he may not be back for a while." Again, everyone laughed. But Ken did reappear after a couple of minutes, looking confounded.

"She disappeared, vanished. The cashier said she saw her go out the front door. I went out the front door. Couldn't have been more than a few seconds behind her, but nothing. Nowhere!"

"She wants to sign on for the trip," Scott said. "Ken is a

little apprehensive and wants to get more information from her... about her. Something. Personally, I think it's some kind of a fluke. She won't show in the morning."

James rises slowly from his chair, walks to the railing and looks down, into the dark water. "She'll be there," he said. His voice sounded very matter-of-fact for a twelve-year-old. Maybe a little too matter-of-fact.

James watches intently as 'something' just beneath the surface of the water in the small marina, swims away.

CHAPTER FIVE

Siren Puts Out To Sea

The following morning was a busy one at the Pier Six Marina, bustling with activity. It was a pastoral morning. There was no wind and therefore no waves on the bay. It was quiet, save for the bumping and thumping of all the dive trip passengers loading baggage and equipment aboard Siren Song, which in the early morning calm seemed loud by contrast.

D J, the deck hand was the busiest person aboard the yacht, stowing everything in its proper place for the trip. This vessel was large enough to have roomy state rooms for its passengers, so a few people were below deck, in their assigned rooms, putting things away. Once that was done, they all seemed to converge in the oversized, broad stern of the craft. Coffee cups were prevalent to accompany the light chatter.

Scott stood away from everyone, checking his camera and capturing a snapshot or two; the first of hundreds he would take on this trip. Angie watched him from several feet away. When Scott Carrington had a camera in his hands, Angie always felt something down deep inside. She was Scott's biggest fan, for she knew the extent of his talent.

Ken Malloy stood on the fantail of the yacht, arms akimbo, hands on his hips, looking around, appearing very much in charge. He glanced at the dock. No one was coming.

"I figured she wouldn't show," Gordon Hughes said. "Probably some gal just pulling our leg for kicks."

"You're probably right. We sure as hell aren't going to wait for her. I didn't really want her anyway. A last minute Lulu. I don't do business that way. Just something strange about her, too. Nothing but trouble and bad luck."

"Aw, don't be so critical. Besides, like I said, she is probably just some bored honey looking for some cheap kicks. On the other hand, there is, after all, an empty stateroom. The charter isn't full."

"Yeah, I know. It never is when we go to The Hole. But I like to have a chance to screen people and check out their credentials before taking them on *any* trip, especially one this long. Actually, most everybody that goes this run has completed a dive class at the Sport Divers of Houston and I kind of know who they are. They don't just show up in a restaurant less than twelve hours before we're due to shove off."

Just at that moment, the door leading into the salon slides open and Maris steps out. Everybody on board looks stunned.

"Hello," Maris says in a very soft, pleasant voice.

Everybody says hello, more than a little surprised, and as if the Maris' greeting was aimed directly at them.

"Where did you come from?" Ken asked.

"I was down below," Maris said sweetly, looking innocent.

"I was just down there. I didn't see you," Ken said, sounding a little irritated.

"Oh! I was way up front, asleep. I didn't know which stateroom would be mine, so I just picked a bench and crashed."

"Asleep? What do you mean, asleep? Did you spend the night here?"

"Well, I wasn't sure what time to be here, and I didn't want to miss the bon voyage."

"Bon voyage? Look, Ma'am,"

"Maris," Maris said, softly, sexy.

"Yeah, okay, Maris. Look, we need to talk. I haven't had a chance to screen you. I haven't even seen your 'C' card. You haven't paid. I don't know what kind of dive equipment you have. This should have all taken place several days ago. Not at the last minute like this."

"My gear bag is stowed below. My 'C' card is there. My money too," Maris said, looking slightly injured.

"Okay, let's go get them and get everything straight," Ken said, as he indicated the doorway. Maris smiled, turned and entered the salon, followed by Ken. As they headed below, Ken can be heard still talking to Maris. "I need to know a lot more about your dive history, where you've been diving, how many dives, how long you've been certified..."

Gordon Hughes, watching them, said to D J, "You may as well cast off. I can tell you in advance what the outcome of *that* conversation is going to be." Then he shook his head ever so slightly. D J smiled and nodded his head, knowingly, then began the process of casting off all lines.

Unfettered, Siren Song gently inches her way out of the

small Pier Six Marina, into the bay. Then, slowly, Captain Hughes increases power, Siren Song begins to roar to life, and heads for the cut through Galveston Island, between Pelican Island and Bolivar Peninsula, leading into the Gulf of Mexico. It is early morning and Siren Song looks very commanding, like a sailor's dream, cutting an arrow straight wake through the table-top still water.

By the time Siren Song reaches the gulf, Maris is on the bow of the yacht, spreading a beach towel to comfortably lie on, applying suntan lotion, a paperback romance novel at her side. She has her hair tied up in a bun, is wearing a 'barely bikini', large sunglasses, and bright red lipstick.

Scott Carrington walks casually about the yacht, his camera in hand, picking up snapshots more than professional photographs. When he finally makes his way forward, toward the bow of the boat, he decides to take a picture, the angle of which catches the bow of Siren Song, contrasted by the morning sun. This photo angle would also reveal Maris, reclined on her beach towel.

He focuses, shoots. Maris apparently hears the click of the camera and is startled. She starts to sit up, turning so that she can see Scott. She seems defensive at first, but quickly puts herself in check, and smiles, then returns to reading her romance novel.

In the wheel room, Captain Gordon Hughes observes the scene on the bow, but says nothing. Sitting opposite the captain is Angie, relaxing in a captain's chair while she smokes a cigarette and watches through the windshield, seeing the same thing that Gordon sees. She watches but says nothing and seems somehow detached from it.

Gordon glances at Angie a quick moment. "Do I sense a hint of jealousy?"

Angie smiles. "Jealousy? Not at all. Scott is his own person. I wouldn't dare do anything to fetter, in any way, that fantastic creative mind of his."

"Sounds like true love," Gordon said.

Angie took a drag on her cigarette and smiled a half smile. "Not really. Maybe. Hell, I don't know. Not the way you mean. I'm in love with his talent, that's for sure. It is a very salable commodity."

"But I thought…"

"Fringe benefits, Mon Capitan. Fringe benefits. I'm Scott Carrington's business partner. Without me, he would probably starve to death, because despite his remarkably amazing talent behind that lens, like so many true artists, he's a lousy businessman. By the same token, without him, I would have to find something else to sell. It's like the bee and the flower. They both need each other. It's a good match-up. We both benefit very well from it. And the fringe benefits just make it all that much sweeter. Him noticing another woman just makes the fringe benefits that much more, 'piquant'. It gives him something to compare me with. Good for my ego because he always comes running back to me after he's sniffed the other flowers. Like I say, it's a good partnership."

"So, what if he didn't?"

"You can't deal with 'what ifs,' Captain. That's a total waste of time. It is what it is, because it is."

Angie looked over at the captain and smiled. He felt like a little bit of Angie had been revealed to him that he hadn't expected. It sure slapped the notion of true romance in the face!

D J and James Harmon have taken chairs at the far stern of the yacht and occupy themselves with the making of decompression lines. Scott has meandered back to that end of the boat and sees the duo talking and laughing with each other. But noise from the large motors drowns out whatever they are saying to each other. DJ says something to James that makes James laugh hard. The scene is relaxed and happy. Scott raises his camera, focuses and takes a picture of the two friends. He checks his window in the camera to make sure it's a clean exposure and is very happy with the picture he has captured.

In the salon, Al Harmon keeps an eye out as Ken Malloy rifles through Maris's scuba gear bag. With a sigh, Ken shakes his head, and stuffs the colorful BC back into the scuba bag, zips it shut and tosses it back into the storage compartment of the boat.

Ken says offhandedly to Al, "Well, she certainly has good enough gear, expensive stuff."

"Okay. So, what's bothering you? Something sure is."

"Damned if I know. I think, her showing up at the very last minute bothers me. And the more I think about it, the more I don't like it because there is something about it that makes me feel like I'm being set up. And then, there's her gear bag. It's all good equipment. Very good, expensive equipment. Doesn't even look like it's been used that much. But none of it is marked. Know what I mean? You know how divers are. They're paranoid about getting things mixed up on a dive, so they mark everything; fins, mask, even their snorkels. And there is *a lot* of equipment in that bag. It's heavy. I don't even know how a little woman like her can lift a bag that big and heavy."

Al chuckled. "Maybe she expects a man to carry it for her."

"Yeah, maybe."

"You checked her 'C' card?"

"Yeah, and there's something screwy about that too."

"In what way?"

"Well, it's very old. The kind that were issued before NAUI started putting people's picture on them. She just doesn't seem old enough to have had a 'C' card that long."

Al nodded agreement.

"If it had rolled over when she was fifteen, it would have to be a photo ID card, assuming she is no older than I think she is."

"And how old do you think that is?" Al asked.

Ken wrinkled his brow. "It's hard for me to tell. I look at her one minute and think she couldn't be more than eighteen. The next time I look at her in a different light, she looks like a minimum of thirty-five, hell, maybe even older."

"You know, something rather strange happened last night while you were gone from the table. Everybody started saying how old she looked to them. Nobody could agree. Gordon called her a child. James thought she was around thirty. Seems like the older a person is, the younger she looks to them. Don't you find that a little weird?"

"Yeah, I do." Ken said. "I don't know. What the hell are we worried about? She's here. She paid for her trip, *in cash*! She may be a little 'different,' but maybe...maybe we just need to relax and enjoy this beautiful day, Siren Song slicing through the water. I'll keep an eye on her when we get wet. If she isn't a good enough diver, I just won't let her go deep, that's all."

Al reflects, thoughtfully. He starts to say something, then doesn't. He just continues to frown. Finally, "Sounds reasonable, I suppose!"

Ken looks at Al and his wrinkled brow. "So?"

"Oh hell, I don't know. Maybe that's the problem. It all sounds so goddamn 'reasonable'. Taking a maiden voyage aboard the Titanic sounded 'reasonable' to more than two thousand people."

The two men chuckle at this in an effort to shake it off and turn their attention to other things.

CHAPTER SIX

The Siren, Revealed

That evening, Al Harmon, Ken Malloy and Scott Carrington are at a table in the lounge of Siren Song playing poker. Angie is there too, but she is stretched out on a couch, asleep. James is in the galley, preparing a sandwich. D J is at the helm, peering unblinkingly at a radar scope as the yacht pushes through the night.

Maris is the loose cannon in this otherwise laid-back scene. She watches everybody intently, especially D J since he is the most alert of the party. She sips from a tea glass, then casually wanders outside the salon, into the stern of the boat, and slides the door closed behind her. Now she is alone in the stern of the yacht. She doesn't waste time looking around, as someone might who is killing time on a long voyage. Instead, she heads for the ladder at the far aft of the stern which leads to the dive platform on the back of the boat.

Maris climbs down the ladder with the glass in her hand, gets down on her knees on the very edge of the platform and dips the glass into the salt spray shooting up from the back of the platform. This would be a dangerous place to be for most people, but Maris doesn't seem concerned.

Once the glass is filled, Maris places the glass to her mouth and drinks thirstily. She breathes heavily for a moment, then fills the glass again and drinks it all. She does this a third time before her thirst seems slaked. She then wets her hand with the saltwater and runs her hand over her face and neck. Her relief is obvious. Fearing to stay longer for danger of being seen, Maris climbs the ladder and takes a seat on one of the lounge chairs in the stern. From there, she stares into the moonlit night at the Zodiac, being towed behind the yacht, making a wake of its own.

It is a good thing for her that no one saw what she did, for then the cat would surely be out of the bag. She relaxes and drifts into sleep, or at least she tries to. Just as she is dozing off, James Harmon slides the salon door open and steps out with his sandwich and a drink. He sees Maris in the lounge chair and decides to sit in the chair next to her. Maris sees him approach and tenses but tries to hide it.

James plops down in the chair next to Maris and says "Hi!" Then takes a bite of his sandwich.

"Hi," Maris says with a feigned smile. A smile not meant to be welcoming. James ignores it.

"Enjoying the trip so far?"

"I suppose," Maris replies as she eyes the youngster.

"Boy, I sure am!" James says. "The Great Blue Hole, huh? That's going to be an exciting dive."

Maris ignores his overture of conversation. "What are you doing here, anyway? Aren't you a little young to run and play with the big dogs? I thought somebody your age was supposed to be in school."

Maris' words seem a little aggressive to James. He eyes

her, but still tries to be friendly, just in case he has misunderstood the intention of her question.

"Early summer vacation. Besides, I just graduated from scuba school. And they thought it would be best for me to get away for a while anyway."

"They?"

"Yeah, people at my high school, and my dad."

"Why did they feel it would be necessary for you to 'get away for a while'?"

"It's kind of an emotional thing." James pauses a few seconds as he studies Maris. Then he decides to push it a little. "It seems like it bothers you that I'm here. Right?"

"Not especially. It just doesn't seem like the place for a twelve-year-old."

"How do you know how old I am? I never told you." James asks.

Maris is caught slightly off guard. "Uh, Scott told me today, sort of in passing."

"Well, anyway, I'm a certified diver. Even though I won't get my regular 'C' card until I'm fifteen."

"Do you even know what 'SCUBA' stands for?"

"Sure. Self Contained Underwater Breathing Apparatus. It's one of the first things you learn in class."

"It also stands for, 'Some Come Up Barely Alive'."

James laughs. "Yeah, I've heard that one too."

"Well, just be careful."

"I will." James continues to eat his sandwich and sip his drink. Maris becomes increasingly agitated at his presence. Suddenly, she turns to him and says somewhat aggressively, "Look, did you have anything specific you wanted to talk about?"

"No," James said, looking at her cautiously now. "I'm just trying to be friendly."

"Well, when you get older, you'll learn that adults like their solitude. Now, if you don't mind..."

James rises from his chair but is surprisingly unhurt by Maris' attack. He starts to walk back inside the lounge, then stops when the salon door is open, turns and looks back at Maris and says, "You know why I'm here, don't you?" With amazing calm, James turns away and enters the salon, sliding the door closed behind him.

Maris looks away from James, but her expression is one of seething hatred.

———

Three days later, Siren Song pulls into the marina at Belize City. It will be necessary for everyone to clear immigration and customs here, get their VISA, etc. Captain Hughes must also secure a permit in order for Siren Song to legally ply the waters of Belize.

In the large immigration office, a couple of dozen people are talking to immigration officers, showing their passports and other documents, all processing into the country. Some people are visitors needing VISAs, some are citizens of Belize, returning to the country from abroad. Everything seems to be going smoothly, at least for a while.

Then Ken Malloy looks across the crowded room and sees Maris being led into an office by an immigration officer. She is carrying her large purse with the strap over the shoulder. The office door closes, and the immigration officer walks back to his post. Ken approaches the officer.

"Excuse me, officer, that lady is with our group. Is there some kind of a problem?

In his thick, Belizian accent, the officer replies, "There is a ques-shan about the lady's passport."

"Oh dear! What kind of question?"

"Well, I'm not supposed to say. But between us, her passport says she was born in 1922."

"Nineteen twenty-two?"

"Yas. I'm sure it's just some kind of a clerical mistake, you know."

"For sure!" Ken says, trying to laugh and make light. "She certainly doesn't look like she was born in 1922 now, does she?"

"No, mahn. That would make her almost one hundred years old. I sure hope I will look that good when I am close to a hundred!" Both men laugh.

"Yeah, if we are lucky enough to live that long," Ken says.

Within a few minutes, the door to the chief immigration officer's office opens and Maris comes out. Ken is watching from across the room, where he has been waiting to see what was going to happen. He watches her movements and expression, but she is impossible to read. Neither body language nor facial expression give away what her emotion might be. She seems neutral.

"What the hell is that?" Ken whispers to himself.

Maris spots him and walks over to where he is leaning against a wall, waiting. "Everything alright?" Ken asks.

"Yeah," she says. "Just some stupid misprint on my passport. Some dizzy bureaucrat put my birthdate in this thing as 1922. Silly. Do I look ninety-eight years old to you?"

"No," Ken says. "But then, I can't tell how old you are. Mind telling me?"

"A lady never tells," Maris says with a dismissive smile, and walks past Ken, toward the dock.

Ken lets her walk away. He continues leaning against the wall, looking at the people in the busy room. But that isn't what he is thinking about. "Something...can't put my finger on it. But something just isn't kosher about that lady. Something..?"

Having cleared customs himself, he turns and walks back to where Siren Song is moored.

CHAPTER SEVEN

Robert's Grove

Once everyone is aboard, having cleared customs and immigration, with their paperwork in hand, Siren Song thunders to life and eases out of port, leaving Belize City behind. Destination, Placencia, on the mainland coast.

Three and a half hours later, Siren Song powers down in the large marina at Robert's grove, Placencia; weaves her way through two large yachts identified by their flag as being from Guatemala, and gently approaches the dock at Robert's Grove Resort. A smiling, middle aged Belizian man named Michael Hooper stands on the pier, waving. Everybody waves back, but especially Gordon, because he knows the man who is a part owner of Robert's Grove. Or at least, he owns stock.

"My main man, Michael!" Gordon says as he hops off the boat onto the dock and shakes hands with Michael. "Good to see you again."

"And you as well," Michael replies. "You look tired and thirsty!"

"It's been a long trip," Gordon says.

As this greeting transpires, D J is busy, responsibly securing Siren Song's lines to the chocks on the pier. He checks twice to make sure each line is secured properly.

"Dr. Maurine got your radio call," Michael says. "All of your rooms are ready, and we're planning a very special dinner tonight. But not here. It will be a camping trip to our little ranch. It's lobster season you know. And when it's lobster season in Belize, we Belizians party and feast on lobsters."

"Couldn't be better!" Gordon said with a big smile. By now, everyone was disembarking. Other helpers were making the boat fast against the dock, although it was a waste of time because D J had done an expert job. By now, D J hopped back on the boat to go inside and kill the engines. For the first time in days, there was no drone of diesels. Siren Song was at peaceful rest.

"Did you stop in Belize City?" Michael asked.

"Oh yeah, of course," Gordon said. "Gotta do the immigration and customs thing, you know."

"Best to keep tings le-gal here in Belize. These local boys never did learn what a sense of humor is." Michael, a typical Belizian, has a beautiful Belize accent. An accent that is a hangover from old English, handed down from long ago when Belize belonged to Great Britain and was known as British Honduras.

"You headed for the Great Blue Hole?"

"Yep, as usual. But after this run, I want to permanently berth Siren Song here."

"Of course, of course. Dr. Maurine tol me. Well, come this way. I'll show each of you to your room." Michael shook hands with everybody as they passed him on the pier.

A greeting and a smile, with the message, "Cocktails await you when you are ready, on the house, of course."

———

Later that afternoon, after going to their respective rooms and freshening up, all members of Siren Song group are sitting around a large table on the deck fronting the bar adjacent to one of the swimming pools. Cocktails are being served, and by now, Dr. Maurine Howard, partner of Robert's Grove Resort, has joined her guests. The conversation is light.

An old man, perhaps in his late seventies, sits far to one side, alone, drinking quietly and looking out at the crystal clear water. He seems to be lost in thought. He says nothing to anyone but has what appears to be a permanent scowl on his face. He is in a wheelchair, which may lend reason for the scowl.

Dr. Howard casually asks Gordon, "How long are you going to be with us this time?"

"I don't know," Gordon answers. "It's up to these fine people. I know we all need a breather from the boat ride. So do I! But then, they're going to want to get on out to The Great Blue Hole. After all, that is their reason for being here."

When the old man at the nearby table hears the words, 'Great Blue Hole', he almost chokes on his drink. He slams his drink down, pushes back from his table and wheels toward Siren Song party. He talks to himself the whole way there. Once there, he says in his old English, Belizian accent,

"The Great Blue Hole, is it? The goddamned, cursed

Great Blue Hole! When will ye ever learn? *She's cursed*, she is! She's inhabited by a blood sucking, evil siren, just waiting to pull men down into her watery bedroom."

The old man points a finger directly at Ken Malloy. "Ye keep goin' down in that hole, young feller, and one day, ye shall not return. It's the God's honest truth I'm a telling ye, and ye know it. If'n ye don't, ye should."

Michael turns to the old man and places his hand on his shoulder, then speaks to him loudly, as if the old man is hard of hearing, which he probably is not. Otherwise, he would never have overheard the conversation at Gordon's table to begin with.

"It's alright now, Mr. Jenkins. Let me send a drink over to your table and I'll warn them about the Great Blue Hole. I promise."

Mr. Jenkins pulls away from Michael. "Humph. I ain't crazy ye know. She damn near killed me once. Woulda got me too, if it hadn't a been fer me lass a swimming down like that and saving me life. Left me in this cursed rolling chair, she did. She devil, that's what. Beware! I know what I'm talking!"

Old man Jenkins backed up and rolled back toward his own table, muttering to himself the whole time. Meanwhile, Michael motioned to the bartender to bring the old man another drink.

"What was that all about?" Angie asked, slightly wide eyed.

Michael spoke softly, so old Jenkins wouldn't hear. "Used to be a coral diver. Black coral was his specialty, deep stuff. His daughter was his crew. Rumors were that there was black coral way down deep inside the Blue Hole. Everybody told him it was bullshit, that it was just folklore, a rumor. But he went in The Hole anyway, looking. The way I heard it he went past the grottos. Was down almost two hundred feet. Had an accident."

"What kind of accident?" Angie asked.

"Dunno for sure. Went too deep, stayed too long. Probably got the raptures. You know, nitrogen narcosis. Well, at that depth, for sure got the raptures. It can make you act crazy if you go deep enough on just regular air. Hallucinate, that kind of stuff. Anyway, his daughter went in after him. Problem was, there wasn't any air left in his tank and he needed to decompress after going so deep. But he couldn't. No air. So, he came straight up to the surface. Got the bends. It put him in that chair."

"Sounds tragic," Angie said with a shiver.

"Unfortunately," Michael continued, "That isn't all there is to the story."

"Oh?"

"Ol' Jenkins, being in the hospital and all, somebody had to keep the business going. At least, his daughter felt that she did. Bills to pay, even here in Belize. And she was the only one to do it. I think she tried to hire divers, but all of them said that if they were going to put their lives in danger and dive deep enough to get black coral, they would do it for themselves, not someone else. So, it was her and her alone. A few days later, a shark attacked her by the wall out there along our great barrier reef."

Michael waves his arm toward the sea.

"Oh my God!" Angie said, horrified. "Killed, or wounded?"

"Killed, in the worst sort of way. The strain was apparently too much for Ol' Jenkins. Loosened up a few screws, if you know what I mean. What you see over there at that table is all that's left."

"So where did he come up with that wild story about a siren?"

"Oh Lord, who knows? Probably a result of the raptures. Being at that depth can make you see some weird things. Can make you *think* some weird things. Worse than that, it can make you *do* some weird things."

Angie shook her head. "I guess so. Still, that's a very tragic story. I guess it can also be a cautionary story to be very careful when you dive that deep."

"This part of the world is filled with, what did you call it? 'Cautionary' stories, Ma'am. Sea tales are forever interlaced with 'cautionary' stories. Some of them are explainable and easy to believe. Some are darker and more mysterious, not so easy to explain. They're harder to believe because we actually don't want to believe them. They're too horrible."

James, sipping on his fruit juice, suddenly spoke up. "You say that like there's truth to those dark and mysterious stories."

"Who knows," Michael said, as he sank into his chair. Fables, legends… There's more of them down here than you could catalog in a lifetime. Greek mythology doesn't have a thing on us. The fact is, there are so many stories that they all get tangled together. It makes it impossible to know truth from fantasy."

"Okay," Angie says, "enough goose bumps."

Everybody laughs. "Yes," Michael says. "Well now, for supper, you are all invited to a Belize style barbeque and camp-out at what we call our 'ranch' only a few kilometers from here. We have transportation waiting, and I promise, the food will be the best you've ever tasted. Spiny lobsters, slow smoked over an open oak fire!"

"Barbequed spiny lobsters?" Al Harmon said. "Well now you're talking. We're all Texans. We *know* about barbeque!"

"Indeed, you do!" Michael agrees. "You Texans have got quite a colorful reputation about things like that. You're going to like this ranch. It was founded by a Texan, sort of a wild man. Believe it or not, he drove the cattle that are on this ranch down here from the Texas border, not by truck, but by horseback."

"Aw yeah," Al Harmon said. "I heard that story. He worked at NASA in Houston, but he as a real rogue. The story I heard was that the trucking company who was supposed to transport the cows through Mexico tried to back him in a corner and overcharge him. He told them something very uncomplimentary about their mothers, unloaded his cattle off the trucks, and took off down the side of the highway. They all said he'd never make it all the way through Mexico. But he was a Texan."

"You're talking about John Mercer. I knew him. And yeah, he was a wild man," Gordon Hughes said with a laugh. They tell a story about somebody taking his parking spot at NASA one day. So, he drove his car up the steps of the building he worked in and parked it on the porch."

Everyone laughs and Gordon continues. "They used to have NASA personnel parties where the rule to get in was that you had to tell at least one John Mercer story. And they were always large parties!" More laughter.

As everyone rose from their chairs at the table and prepared to load up for the ride to the ranch, Gordon Hughes turned to D J and said, "D J, I'm sorry, but I'm going to have to ask you to stay behind. You know the policy about leaving the boat unguarded."

"Sure, no problem," D J said. "Just bring me a lobster when you come back in the morning."

"Let him come with us," Scott Carrington said.

"No, it's alright," D J countered. "Rules are rules for a reason. Besides, I've been to that ranch before, and with all due respect to Mr. Hooper, the beds on Siren Song are a lot more comfortable. I'm talking, a *lot* more comfortable."

Maris looks mildly alarmed. "Oh! We're going to spend the night? The whole night? I need to run to the boat and get a couple of things."

Actually, almost everyone has to return to Siren Song to collect one thing or the other. Everyone is below deck except Maris who quickly descends the stern ladder to the dive platform, again with glass in hand and a plastic milk carton with a screw-on top tucked under her arm. She quickly dips the glass in the sea water and drinks deeply, once, twice, and finally three times. Then she dips the plastic milk carton in the water, fills it, caps it. Thus done, she scampers up the ladder and tucks the filled carton in a tote bag which she places on a chair.

Her timing is close. Just as she completes her task, other members of the party begin to appear from below deck with their own totes, or small bags with overnight necessities. The chatter is light and happy as everyone tells D J goodnight and how much they will miss him at the party on the ranch. Gordon Hughes promises to bring D J a barbequed lobster.

D J's parting words as the group make their way up the pier are, "Don't worry about me. I'm going ashore long enough to get dinner. Besides, look at it this way; me, here, with an eighty-foot yacht. You might be surprised at how much 'company' I can come up with!"

Hearing his words, Angie turns and waves bye-bye to him. "With your good looks, I wouldn't doubt it!" she says with a soft laugh. Then she turns back and joins the group. Dr. Maurine Howard is standing where the pier meets the bulkhead. She smiles and wishes everyone a good time on the ranch.

CHAPTER EIGHT

D J is Missing!

The dive party bounces down a curvy, dusty dirt road that wends its way through tropical low-land jungle. The vehicle is the lodge's extended length large Nissan Van, outfitted for up to twelve passengers.

Michael is driving. Sitting next to him is Maris and on the passenger side is Al Harmon. Michael brags about his country as they drive along.

"We've got some of the most tropical jungle to be found anywhere, right here in Belize. Lots of mahogany, sapodilla and rubber trees, Lots of chicle trees. That's because we have good climate and fertile soil. We also have a good forestry service that closely regulates the number of trees which can be harvested each year, and they mean it. That's the reason so many people, including me, grow sugar cane here. You know, Belize gained its independence from Great Britain back in 1981. Since then, all sorts of economic opportunities have come to our country."

Give me an example," Al said.

"Investment money is more readily available. Enough

where a person with ambi-shan can do things. I myself am going to diversify. My plantation is doing well. I have stock in Robert's Grove Resort, and the tourist industry is doing well. You, for instance are going to start berthing Siren Song at our resort. You'll be able to stay booked if you want. Hell, maybe even buy a house and move down here! Make many trips to The Great Blue Hole. We're only about forty miles from it as the crow flies, as you know."

"Yes, that's one reason I want to berth at Robert's Grove."

Nobody was watching as Maris expression turned more and more angry. She stayed silent, but the fury was there.

Michael continued with a big smile on his face. "I might even go into compete-shan with you and start booking trips to The Hole."

"Ah well, there's room for everybody. I think we could help each other with a project like that." Al said.

"I would like that very much," Michael said.

"I also have a little money that I might be interested in investing here in Belize. Maybe you and I can get our heads together and you can point me to some good deals."

"I would love to!" Michael said with a smile.

Just then, Michael hits a particularly deep pothole. The large Nissan Van lurches to the left. Everyone's gear which is stowed in the back of the large vehicle, gets jostled. This includes Maris' tote bag. The milk carton in her tote tips over and the top, which she did not screw on tightly, manages to come off. The water in the container quickly spills.

Minutes later, they reach the ranch house. Everybody piles out, a little worse for wear due to the heat and dust, but Maris is sweating profusely, and seems to be suffering. As the luggage is unloaded by a ranch hand, Maris searches frantically for her tote, and then her jug of water. She could even drink from the milk container in front of everybody, and nobody would know the difference. They would never suspect she had sea water in the container. Then, finding the top off of her container, and discovering that the water spilled, she can hardly contain herself. Maris hits the panic button.

She marches stiffly up to Michael and says, "I have to go back to the resort."

Michael looks at her, shocked. "What?"

"I have to go back. I really have to go back. I just realized, I forgot my medicine and I simply can't do without it. I'm very sorry."

"It's not a problem," Michael says. I'll just phone the resort, have somebody retrieve your medicine and bring it to us."

"No," Maris says in a near panic. "They wouldn't know where to look, would never find it. I've got to go back, *now!*"

Anxious to accommodate, Michael says, "Okay. Well don't worry, I'll have Tontoni, that ranch hand over there, drive you back right away."

Michael walks over to where the ranch hand is standing and instructs him to drive the distraught Maris back to Robert's Grove. While he is busy doing that, Angie pulls Maris to one side.

"What's going on with you, Maris? I've been with you for the past three days, and I haven't seen you taking medication of any kind whatsoever."

Maris searches quickly for a plausible excuse. "That letch pinched me on the butt all the way out here. I'm sorry, but I just don't want to spend the night in the same house with him."

Angie is momentarily taken off guard. She looks in the direction of Michael. "Michael? He doesn't seem like that kind of person to me. Besides, I don't know how he could have pinched you on anything. He was hanging on to the steering wheel with both hands the whole time."

"You can believe what you want to believe. I was sitting next to him and he's a letch, I tell you. I just want out of here as fast as possible."

Angie eyed Maris suspiciously. "Uh huh. Okay. I guess we'll see you back at the boat tomorrow."

Maris very acidly says, "Whatever," then turns to get in the Nissan Van. Tontoni slides into the driver's seat. Michael walks around to the passenger side and places his hand on Maris' shoulder as he says, "Well, it was nice getting to meet you. Have a safe trip back to the lodge. I'll call them and let them know you're coming so they can have supper ready for you by the time you get there."

"Fine," Maris says as she looks down at the floorboard of the vehicle.

Angie watches this exchange very closely to see if there was any indication suggestive or otherwise insidious in Michael's actions. But she sees nothing remotely inappropriate, that would suggest anything.

"That little bitch is a liar," Angie said to herself, under her breath, at the same time, wondering what it was that Maris was really up to.

Michael motions to Tontoni, who cranks up the van and they're off in a cloud of dust.

Less than forty-five minutes later, Tontoni pulls into the parking area of Robert's Grove and Maris hops out, quickly grabs her things from the back of the van, thanks Tontoni and rushes away at a half run toward the pier, and Siren Song. Tontoni waves goodbye to her back, then backs up and drives away.

Maris hops aboard Siren Song and sprints below deck, calling for D J. Receiving no response in that part of the boat, she returns on deck, this time with her glass in her hand. She looks around again, very carefully, to make sure D J, or for that matter, no-one else, is in sight. Then she descends the stern ladder to the dive platform, gets down on her knees and dips the glass into the water. It is obvious that she is badly stressed as she drinks and keeps drinking several glasses of sea water before stopping to breathe heavily and catch her breath.

Although she is dressed in shorts, she decides to sit on the dive platform and hang her feet off the back. This gets her shorts wet, but she doesn't seem to mind at all.

She decides to slide back a couple of feet so that she can lean her back against the transom of the boat. She takes a deep breath, leans her head back and closes her eyes. After a few moments, she leans forward and dips her glass into the water again, placing the glass to her mouth and drinks.

At that moment, some kind of movement catches her eye, and she turns to see D J standing on the pier, looking down at her. D J looks shocked. He holds a beer in his hand but doesn't appear to be inebriated. Although it is now dark, there are lights on the pier, and he is sure he cannot be mistaken. Maris was drinking sea water. His presence shocks Maris. She had obviously not heard his approach.

But her shock is nothing compared to D J's.

"Maris? What are you doing back here so soon? And what in the hell are you doing dinking sea water?"

"I wasn't actually drinking it. I was gargling with some to get a bad taste out of my mouth."

"I've never seen anybody gargle with sea water. And in any case, you were swallowing."

Maris giggles. "Okay, you caught me. I was experimenting."

"Experimenting?"

"I read somewhere that old sailors, lost at sea, could have actually drank sea water to survive if they had wanted to. I've been drinking a little tonight, and I don't mean water. So, I decided to put it to a test. Crazy, I know."

"Well I don't know where you read that, but it's wrong. You can't drink sea water. It'll make you sick as hell and you'll either up-chuck or it'll make you crazy as a bed bug."

Maris' eyes start to flash with contempt, but then she gets control of herself.

"It's okay. Forget about all that and come sit beside me," she says, as she begins to remove her blouse. "I'm just glad we finally have a chance to be alone. I've been watching you, you know."

D J looks appreciatively at Maris large, perfectly formed breasts with large areoles. She smiles up at him, then reaches her arm toward him as she says, "Come on."

D J looks tempted, but then draws back and says, "I don't think I'd better. You're a client. That's a no-no. I'm not supposed to go swimming close to the pier anyway and besides, there's just *something* about you that is too weird. So, thanks, but no thanks."

Maris, nude from the waist up, slides off of the dive platform into the water. D J has been watching all of this intently, but now turns to walk away. That's when the sound starts.

The sound is like the voice of an angel singing, supported by a lyre. D J struggles but cannot walk away. He hears Maris call his name. "Come to me, D J. Come swimming with me."

Unable to resist, D J turns back toward her, but stands on the pier. Maris throws her shorts and whatever else she was wearing below the waist onto the dive platform. D J, looking hypnotized, unbuttons his shirt and tosses it onto the deck of Siren Song. It is quickly followed by the rest of his clothing. He steps down onto the fantail of the yacht, then climbs the ladder down to the dive platform, and from there, slides into the water where Maris awaits.

She smiles a seductive smile as she moves through the water toward him. She wraps her arms and legs around him and places her mouth on his for what presumably will be a passionate kiss; and it is, at first. But Maris' kiss turns onto something else as she pulls D J beneath the surface of the water and refuses to remove her mouth so he can get a breath of air.

Indeed, she begins to suck the air out of him. As she exhales, bubbles float to the surface. D J struggles desperately, but it is hopeless. Maris has him in her grasp, and once again she places her mouth upon his to suck what little air he has remaining in his lungs out of him. D J is frantic. He fights to free himself from the grip of this she devil, but he needs air, and there is none. Maris has made sure of that. She smiles at him as he blacks out and drowns.

The struggle is over. D J is no more. And now, Maris performs her most grotesque of deeds. She transforms into her true self. Her face changes into that of a sea creature with razor sharp, long, fang-like teeth. The pupils of her eyes are elliptical. And, on her head, instead of hair, she has tentacles.

She assaults the dead body of D J, opening her gaping maw and taking D J's face into it, then biting down, hard. The water is suddenly clouded with blood. Again and again she strikes, ripping pieces of D J's face and head into small pieces and devouring them.

Several minutes later, Maris resurfaces, but by now, she has morphed back into a beautiful, but naked woman. She looks down at the pile of clothes on the dive platform, puts her clothes on, and throws D J clothes into the water. Then, very calmly, she walks through the salon, to below deck in Siren Song for the night.

CHAPTER NINE

At the Ranch

It is night-time, at the ranch, approximately the same time as Maris has committed murder behind Siren Song. The promised delicious, barbequed lobster dinner did not disappoint. It has been finished and the guests are sitting around a big campfire in folding chairs, sipping brandy and swapping stories.

Everyone that is except for James Harmon. He has become fascinated with some books he has found on the shelves in the ranch house library. As he peruses the shelves, he comes across a book entitled, *Folklore of the Caribbean*.

This immediately captures the young man's attention. He pulls it from the shelf and begins perusing through it.

Angie, a little bored with the man talk around the campfire, has left the circle and come into the ranch house for a visit to the girl's room. Upon leaving there, she spots James in the library and wanders in.

"Whatcha doing there, Big Boy?" she says with a smile.

"Just fooling around with these dusty ol' books," James replies. "I found one about *Folklore of The Caribbean*."

"Oh yeah? Anything interesting in it?"

"Maybe. Listen to this. It's about the Sirens of Anthemoessa. That's an island off the coast of Italy that is talked about in the Jason and The Argonauts story. Problem is the island only exists in myth."

"Wait a minute. I thought you said it was folklore of the Caribbean."

"Yeah, but all oceans are tied together. So, there's bound to be some kind of a connection. Anyway, 'All three sirens mated and bore young. But it was Leucosia who took as a mate, Gonak, the sea monster. Their mating resulted in the birth of a female child whom they named after the sea. Unlike her mother, the child could not drown beneath the waves. Instead, she dwelled there at her father's side until she was of age. A 'sea creature' named Onash banned the child from the Mediterranean. Onash cast her out because of his jealousy of Gonak. For Onash had been eternally in love with Leucosia and felt the child should have been his.'

"'Onash, being the stronger and having more power, than Gonak, Gonak was left with no other choice. He was told he must either remove his daughter from the Mediterranean or she would be killed. So, it came to pass that her father delivered her to a place where he said she would find 'eternal clear waters and a sanctuary to call hers alone.' That place came to be far away from the Mediterranean, in a sea called the Caribbean. There, the child became ensconced, within a giant reef in which...get this...'there exists a chamber befitting such a royal heiress.' Royal? Since when is a sea creature royal? And howcum somebody would suggest that when they wrote about her?"

"Wait! Back up. 'Chamber'? So, what are you suggesting? The Great Blue Hole?"

"Maybe. But remember, this is all supposed to be bullsh... I mean, mythology. Continuing, 'The child, her exact name unknown, inherited certain powers from each of her parents, though not all from either. It is said she can call men with enchanting song, as did her mother, but devour them as did her father, once she has drawn them down into the sea.'

"'Her powers are very limited. It is said, for instance, that she can only lure men *one at a time*, not an entire ship's company, such as the original three sirens did.'

"Yeah, I remember from reading Jason and the Argonauts that the three sirens sang like angels and made men lose their wills. The sailors crashed ships onto the reef surrounding Anthemoessa, and the sailors on those ships wasted away on the island. 'The beaches turned white with the bleaching bones of dead sailors.' Boy, that must have been some kind of singing!"

"Better than the Bee Gees!"

"Oh, hell no! Nothing is better than the Bee Gees!"

"So, what was the deal with Jason and The Argonauts?"

"Greek Mythology: Jason had heard about how beautiful the sirens' singing was, and wanted to hear it, but not at the expense of losing his ship, the Argo. So, he instructed his sailors to tie him to the mainmast of the ship, then every sailor on board was ordered to fill their ears with wax, so they couldn't hear, then sail past the sirens' island. That way, Jason got to hear the sirens sing, all he wanted to. That must have really pissed off the sirens! There's nothing a singer hates worse than an indifferent audience!"

"Jason was a pretty smart guy."

"You think? Anyway, back to this bit about Leucosia's daughter. 'She cannot control women at all, nor a male child younger than the age of puberty. This, because her power depends on her ability to appeal to the male's sexual lust. But beware the siren because she has the ability to call upon sea creatures for assistance and most deceitfully, she can change appearance at will. If she is unable to lure the young with sexual desire, she is apt to attack them in her true form and feed upon their flesh and bones.'

"Damn! Hasn't this broad ever heard of McDonalds? She needs to lighten up. Okay, going on... 'It is said she has a sister who takes on more the form of their mother, with the face and breasts of a woman, but the body, wings and feet of a bird. And who, so equipped, can fly as well as swim. But this is little more than rumor. No sailor has ever spake of her in their spinning of tales and there is only one reference to her in the annals of mythology.' A sister? This is getting worse! A sister! Okay, back to the book.

"'It is of no matter. It is the daughter named after the sea whom sailors speak of with dread. It is also said that she demands solitude and becomes enraged at what she considers trespassers. It is further rumored that her lair lies within a place called Lighthouse Reef, in the western Caribbean. Evidence of this is the high number of ships that have crashed against the barrier of the reef, despite the presence of a good and functioning lighthouse. Lighthouse Reef is located within the territorial limits of a Central American country known as British Honduras. Above all, heed ye her as a danger to life, lest ye ever be confronted by her in disguise.'"

James looks from the book, up to Angie. Then back at the book. "There's more, 'She can take on the form of a beautiful woman at will. But must never leave the sea for more than a short time, for she has gills that are secreted deep within her throat that must be constantly wetted with sea water.'"

James closes the book. "Whew!"

"What do you think?" Angie asks.

"I think I'm going to need your help with something," James says. "If there's anything about this book that isn't pure fantasy, if there is any truth to it at all, you are the only other person besides me that this broad can't mesmerize."

"What are you saying, James?"

"Me and you, Ms. Holland. Me and you."

"Let's keep this in perspective, Tiger," Angie says. "This is, after all, a book of mythology. And not a very well written book at that. From the verbiage, it sounds to me like there might have been a little bit of, 'Yo-ho-ho, and more than one bottle of rum' involved. And as far as I'm concerned, that goes to credibility. I'll give you that some of these circumstances seem, on the surface to...oh hell! Just out of curiosity... I mean, you aren't trying to suggest that our passenger, Maris, is a siren...are you? I mean, that's not even on your mind...is it?"

"If the shoe fits. Her name is Maris, which is Latin for Sea. I know, I checked. She shows up out of nowhere the night before we're scheduled to shove off. She gives Captain Hughes the bum's rush. After she leaves our table, no one can agree on whether she's a blond or brunette, whether she's eighteen, or thirty-five. She comes on to me as fakey nice."

"Fakey?"

"Yeah, fakey. It's a kid word. Deal with it. Fakey is like

politicians do. It's all put on, highly refined, one hundred percent pure, unadulterated bullshit."

Angie leans back and takes a deep breath. "Wow! I hear what you're saying, but come on, James, this is the twenty-first century. Sirens? Sea Monsters? It's fun to talk about around the campfire, but I don't think... I mean, granted, she is a strange person, and I don't like her very much. But..."

"For the sake of our survival, you need to start thinking differently. Consider the possibility."

"No, Honey, you need to. Things written in that book simply do not exist. Your thinking could be very dangerous. First of all, if you begin to let yourself believe that stuff, you're not going to enjoy this wonderful trip, and that would be a shame. There are many legends about the Great Blue Hole. I read one about some green monster with red eyes and a slashing tail that lives in the bottom of the hole. But that one is no more real than this one about a siren. It's fun to imagine, to play around with. You know, I would like for Peter Pan to be real. But he isn't. Sorry. Well, actually I'm kind of glad where your siren is concerned." Angie tries to change the subject.

"Wouldn't you like to go outside by the fire? Maybe cook a smoors? I'll join you. God! I haven't had a smoors since I was a girl scout."

James ignores Angie's invitation, shakes his head and looks down at the floor for a moment. Then he looks back at Angie. "Okay. She's not real. But it's a long evening and we don't have a television set, so humor me for a short minute, and let's pretend."

Angie thinks about it for a minute, then reaches out and takes James' hand. "Okay, what the hell. Let's pretend."

"Okay. We're living in Never-Never Land see, like Peter Pan. And sirens really do exist, like the one that supposedly killed my great-great grandfather."

"What? Wait a second! I hadn't heard about that."

"I'll tell you later. Now, stay with me. Okay, 'pretend' you are a sea siren, and like a lot of other wild creatures on this earth, you feel like your habitat is being encroached upon. You can do this because unlike most 'creatures' you have the ability to think. Your secret hiding place, your 'home' that has been sacred for nearly two thousand years suddenly becomes a playground for a bunch of asshole sport divers. You live deep underwater, but every once in a while, you look up and see a beer can floating down from the surface. Or worse, it lands right beside you. Imagine your reaction. Indignant outrage? Now consider your inherent instincts and tell me, what would you do? Think hard about it because remember, we're playing pretend, so no barriers. And since we don't have any TV, we're gonna make our own TV show. Now, go!"

Angie smiles. She is still holding James' hand. "My! What a mind you have for a twelve-year-old. Well, let me see. I suppose if I were becoming an endangered species, I would strike back at whatever was endangering me."

"Bingo! Of course you would. Survival would demand it. You say that rather off-handedly, but you're right on target. Now, let's take it a step farther. Creatures in mythology were seldom if ever dummies. And it only figures that a female anything trying to be an enchantress would have to be educated, right?"

"Where are you going with this, James?"

"Just stay with me. So, it's a fair assumption that a siren would be able to read, right?"

"I hadn't thought about it, but I suppose so."

"Now, what we don't know why a siren would be tolerant enough to endure even one invasion into her domain, let alone several. Maybe there were too many divers. Remember, that book said that this siren can only entrance one person at a time, and no women at all. Or, maybe at first, she was frightened. I can imagine that seeing a person wearing all that equipment would frighten you, if you didn't know what it was. Maybe there were women *and,* maybe kids along, like me. Anyway, for whatever reason, she didn't bug 'em. But...let's say she followed them to the surface long enough to see them pulling away in their boat. And more than once she saw the same name on the transom.

"Siren Song!"

"Right again. So, being the intelligent sea monster, she devises a plan. She gets it in her head that if she can wipe out just one or two dive parties, she'll scare hell out of anybody else who gets a weed up their... I'm sorry. I mean, a desire to dive her lair, The Great Blue Hole. I mean, it's not like the Great Blue Hole is just around the corner from the soda shop anyway. And British Honduras is no longer British Honduras; it's now Belize, as you know. Problem is Belize has been independent since 1981 and in that time they have pushed hard for tourism according to what my dad tells me. So I did a little research. What does Belize have to offer, really? A little bit of gambling, but who cares? A jungle tour up the Belize River? Boring! A few Mayan ruins. But mostly, fishing and scuba diving. What are the best places to dive? The Great Barrier Reef and the Great Blue Hole.

"More and more, our she-monster has had to duck and

hide. I don't know about you, but I'd sure get pissed off if people kept coming into my living room un-invited. And it's not as if she can open a gift shop down there."

Angie chuckles, "James! I do admire your mind. I hope *if I ever* have a child, they are as precocious as you are. You are amazing."

"Thanks. But right now, we need to get our heads together because if I'm right, and I'm pretty sure that I am, we're dealing with a creature who is determined to kill every last person aboard Siren Song, including you and me."

This statement brings Angie to a halt for a minute. She tries to conceal the fear in her eyes by changing the subject.

"There's more danger than that afoot. That Belizian out there is selling your father on some laurel-wood dream about making money in Belize through investments. Your dad is definitely being set up."

"I don't think so. Michael seems like a sincere person. Besides, don't worry about my dad. He can take care of himself. Right now, I want to focus on the problem at hand."

"Alright. I must say, James, you spin one hell of a story. But okay, let's say you're on to something... pretending, of course."

"Whatever you say. Let's hope I am."

"Why should she come all the way to the Texas coast looking for us? That seems like an awful lot of trouble when she could just stay at The Great Blue Hole and wait for Siren Song to return."

"I've thought about that and it bamboozeled me at first. But if she is as calculating as I think she is, she is going to want to find out all she can about who we are. Me, for instance. I'm a kid. I'm a big problem to her. You are a woman. Problem. Everybody else on the boat is easy picking. But she wouldn't have known that without coming to the starting point to do some recon. She has to kill us. Doesn't have a choice in her mind. She has to frighten people away from the Great Blue Hole. More tourists mean more scuba divers. With all of the new, high tech equipment, scuba diving is the in thing. So, more excursions to the Great Blue Hole, and Maris knows it. Unless.."

"The Great Blue Hole gets a reputation not unlike the Bermuda Triangle, only more intense."

"You're starting to catch on. We've got to prevent a lot of murders, starting with ours."

"Murders! You're some kid. I swear, at this point you've almost got me convinced. But maybe you would do better if you're thinking was in bed. Isn't it about bedtime for a young man like you?"

"Yes, ma'am. Just tell me one thing, what would you do if Maris really turns out to be a siren?"

"I... I don't know."

"Would you help me kill her?"

"James, that's too horrible to think about. Besides, how do you know a siren can be killed?"

"I don't. But I have this feeling we may have to find out. Good night, Ms. Holland."

James turns and walks outside and say goodnight to everyone. Angie doesn't move, except for her hand. She reaches for the old book about 'Folklore of The Caribbean.'

CHAPTER TEN

A Sleepless Night

In the ranch house, at two in the morning, a shadowy figure moves silently across the bedroom where James Harmon is sleeping and stands next to his bed. It is a female figure. She bends over as her hand reaches out, toward James' throat. But it is not his throat she wants to touch. It is his shoulder. The shadowy figure is Angie. She shakes James gently, then sits on the bed beside him. He wakes and sits up, wondering what she is doing there.

Without formality, Angie says, "James, in your opinion, how do you fit into such a bizarre picture? I mean, is it just an accident of timing? Or is there something more?"

"I'm not sure. I think it's just random. She isn't after anyone in particular. She just wants to wipe out a bunch of people and create fear of The Great Blue Hole. But 'if' it's something personal, then I think it has something to do with my great-great grandfather."

"How?"

"Well, tell me something, Ms. Holland, are you a

religious person? That is, do you believe in the spirit world?"

"I believe in a supreme being, if that's what you mean."

"Supreme being equals spirits, right? I mean, if there's a supreme being, then there is a hereafter."

"Yes, that's right."

"And who lives in the hereafter if spirits don't?"

"Yes, of course. What are you driving at?"

"What I'm driving at is, our family is very big on tradition, ancestral history and all that stuff. According to ordinance, all the men in our family are, or have been, 'men of the sea', whether they wanted to be or not. Now if it's true about spirits, then it's got to also be true about monsters."

"Not necessarily but do go on."

"Try it on for size anyway. I'm still trying to make my point. There's an old family legend passed down about my great-great grandfather. Like all of us, he was 'a man of the sea'. According to this legend, he was apparently hauling silver out of Merida, Yucatan, headed for Spain, when the ship got caught in a storm. Well, Grandpa was a slyer than usual old fox and he cut east, through the Yucatan Channel. I guess he figured if he went in the direction the storm was coming from, he'd sail out of it quicker. And it worked!

"He managed to escape the fury of the storm. But as it turned out, that wasn't good enough to save his ship and his men. They got down in this area somewhere and went aground on an atoll. Great-great Grampa was helping his men into lifeboats when he heard something. His men heard it too, but they weren't affected by it the way he was. Then, according to the story the survivors told, a beautiful woman came up out of the sea and sang directed to my great-great grandfather, right there in the middle of the storm and everything. They tried to tell him it wasn't a real woman, but a She Devil in disguise. But their warnings didn't do any good. It seemed like he was hypnotized or something. The last they saw of him, the She Devil had her arms wrapped around him and was pulling him under water. That was all she wrote. They never saw him again.

"Then, another storm was whipping out of the north at that point and the survivors' lifeboats came aground along the coast of Honduras. They weren't able to chart anything about where the ship had gone down, but I'm willing to bet, it was right out there on Lighthouse Reef."

"What do you plan on doing, looking for the wreck?"

"Not hardly. The water surrounding Lighthouse Reef is over six thousand feet deep."

"Then what, James? What are you really doing here?"

"Strange as it may sound, I think I'm here to fulfill some destiny, set up by this fancy heritage of mine. I wouldn't think so, but something happened to me a couple of weeks ago at school. It was like I was being called by someone. 'If' spirits exist, then my great-great grandfather is out there somewhere and he thinks, or knows, the same siren that nailed him is about to go on a full-scale rampage. I think he wants me to stop it."

"Why you?"

"Did you read that book? You were looking at it when I came back inside. According to what it says, she doesn't have any power over me because I'm not old enough to... you know."

"I know. But I also know, when you are, *all* the beautiful women in this world had better look out." Angie smiled in the dark, as she ruffled James' hair.

"Apparently that time isn't very far away. Just between you and me, I think the whole thing has to do with timing. Who else in our family can great-great-Grampa recruit? The siren is fixing to go bananas and I'm the only male Harmon still young enough to deal with her. I know that sounds like one hell of a qualification for a job like killing somebody, and I'm not crazy about the whole thing. But there it is."

Angie is quiet for along minute. Then, "James, I've said it before. You're the most remarkable twelve-year-old I've ever met in my life. Either you're right, and you are a natural born investigator, or you have the damdest imagination of any kid in the world."

"Which one do you think it is?"

"I wish I knew. I know one thing, you've managed to scare the hell out of me!"

"But the truth is, you don't think it's all imagination, do you?"

Angie looked down and shook her head. "No, Tiger, I don't. Don't ask me why. This has got to be the most bizarre, the most outlandish thing I have ever heard. But... something, way down deep inside of me says to put aside everything I've ever known or believed about logic and team up with a twelve-year-old boy. True, a precocious boy, but a boy."

James gets out of bed and puts his arms around Angie and gives her a hug. Angie hugs James back, but looks into the darkness and continues to talk.

"For what it's worth, I think I might have come up with a theory about why she surfaced in Texas." Then Angie half giggled. "'Surfaced!' Now there is an apropos word if ever there was one."

"Really!"

"Now James, assuming that all of this doesn't turn out to be pure bull, put yourself in her shoes and it isn't too hard to see. It's far easier to attack from the inside, especially if you know your own weaknesses. I'm referring to her inability to control your pre-pubescent mind. So, it would make sense for her to want to start from the beginning and choose her victims carefully. Plan a strategy of some kind."

"That's what I've been saying, just in different words."

"In that case, you and I would be her two main enemies."

"Precisely."

"But she hasn't been all that bad to me...yet. Sometimes I have a little trouble collecting my thoughts when I'm around her. What do you think? Some kind of a jamming system to throw me off guard?"

"Probably."

"How has she treated you so far?"

"Terrible. She hates my guts. I put that theory to the test the first night out from San Leon."

"Hmmm. Alright, Kiddo. I'm joining your team, but with one understanding."

"Which is?"

"No matter how sure we are of ourselves, we're still operating on some very circumstantial evidence here, and you're talking about taking some extreme corrective measures. My deal is, for now, let's watch and *only* watch. That means, we also don't burden anyone else with what we think we know unless and until it comes down to showtime."

"Yeah, I guess that would probably be best. I wanted to talk to my dad about it, but that may not be a good idea, yet."

James shakes hands with Angie in the dark. "You've got a deal."

"Remember Sweetheart, we've got to give her every benefit of the doubt. And considering how you, well, how both of us feel, that isn't going to be easy."

"I know," James says. His trembling voice reveals his nervousness.

"There is a possibility that all we're dealing with here is a rather strange girl whose worst sin is, well, being a little too sexy."

"You don't believe that any more than I do."

"You're right, I don't. But James, this is all so crazy. What if it turns out to be real, we get our backs against the wall and then, we can't kill her?"

"Oh, that's simple. She'll kill *us*."

James says this a little too matter of factly for Angie, and she starts slightly. Then James smiles. He then sits on the bed beside Angie.

"How did I get tangled up in this? I'm twelve years old. I should be worrying about riding my bicycle, and how to cheat on my arithmetic test. Watching my pet hamster run in a wheel. Not plotting the real murder of a mythological creature."

Angie puts her arm around James and pulls him to her in a protective, motherly way. "I know. It's too much responsibility to put on anybody. Much less somebody your age."

"The thing that drives me is this; If everything we've talked about is true, then it is just as true that my great-great-grampa sent me here. I don't think he'd do that if he didn't know something that we don't know."

Angie thinks about James' words for a minute. "Don't ask me why, but that makes sense, somehow."

Angie gets up, kisses James on the cheek and runs her fingers through his hair. "Try to get a little more sleep." She then turns and walks away, shoulders slightly bent in her night-robe.

"Yeah, you too," James says with a half-smile.

"Sure," Angie says, over her shoulder. "I'm going to sleep like a baby. Uh-hum!"

CHAPTER ELEVEN

Halfmoon Caye

It is mid-morning at Robert's Grove. Al Harmon and Gordon Hughes are standing on the pier adjacent to Siren Song, talking, and looking worried. There is music, and the sound of parade drums coming from somewhere on shore. A celebration is in progress, although the purpose of it is yet unclear to Al and Gordon.

"In dis paht of the worl, dey call it a 'jump up'," one of the resort workers explained when Al Harmon asked. "June is de middle of lobstah season in Belize. We have all kinds of lobstah festivals."

The two men walked toward the dock, then onto land when they see James appear from a group of people who have formed themselves into a parade.

"Did you find him?" Al Harmon asks.

"No, but some waitresses at a bar over there by the harbor called 'The Coral Reef' said he was there last night, talking to a couple of girls."

"Ah ha!" Gordon said. "Wait! There's a bar open this time of morning?"

"Yeah, there's some kind of a lobster fiesta cranking up. I guess these people take their celebrations pretty seriously. Anyway, the waitresses said that D J seemed to be, 'making a good time, mahn!'"

Gordon guffawed. "Yeah, he did hint that he might 'entertain himself', didn't he? Looks like he might have gotten lucky."

"You might say that." Al agreed. "Oh, to be young again!"

"What do you mean, 'got lucky'?" James asked.

"I'll explain it some other time," Al said with a smile. "Like, when you're seventeen, if you haven't figured it out by then."

"Ohhh," James said, nodding his head and smiling. "You're saying he got to bingo with one of those girls."

"Yep. With one or more."

"Precocious kid!" Gordon Hughes says with a smile. "But you'd think D J would have brought a 'guest' back to the boat to entertain her."

"Seems like it. But look around. It's lobster fiesta time. He probably got talked into going to a party somewhere. You can bet a pretty penny that he's shacked up somewhere, probably with a terrible hangover."

Gordon shook his head. "That's still pretty irresponsible of him. He knows we have a dive trip shoving off this morning."

"Nothing's missing from the boat, is it?"

"No, and Maris said she's been here ever since she returned from the ranch. Nobody was here when she arrived last evening."

"Yeah, well, now we know why. With Maris on board, D

J wouldn't have wanted to bring some broad here. It could have gotten awkward."

"You mean, she'd be in the way of him putting the move on some innocent Belizian."

"Well, Belizian maybe. Not so sure about innocent."

Just at that moment, Michael walks up and joins them. A costumed jump-up band is marching past the resort. The drums and cymbals are very cacophonous, so Michael has to talk loudly.

"I've checked with the police and the hospital. He isn't in either one of those places. Didn't he do this one time before?"

"Yeah," Gordon said, slightly angry. "Same scenario. We had a trip planned to the Great Blue Hole. He didn't show up until noon, and looked like death warmed over. Wasn't worth a damn to me all day. I didn't fire him because I like him and most of the time, he's a damn good deck hand. He's also a diver and understands what kind of things to do when people are gearing up. But this really pisses me off."

"What do you want to do?" Michael asks.

"I don't know. What can we do? We're going to have to wait for him. Shit! Let's go watch the parade. You say this is a lobster festival they're celebrating?"

"That's right. They're getting an early start this early in the morning!" Michael laughs knowingly.

Getting his meaning, everyone laughs as they walk toward the street where the parade is passing.

"What the hell!" Al Harmon says, "We might as well get in on this 'jump up'. It would be a shame if everybody had a good time except us."

"That's right," Gordon says. "I want to get just drunk enough to beat D Js ass when he finally shows up."

"Can I help with that?" James says.

"Absolutely," Gordon says with a smile as they catch up to the revelers. All three of them fall into line and try to imitate the celebration dance. Their beginning try is only 'so-so', but no matter. They're having a good time.

———

At dawn the following morning, Gordon Hughes stands on the stern deck of Siren Song, looking toward shore. Michael is there with him.

"This is ridiculous," Gordon says. "That young-un should have been back by now, no matter where he went. What in the hell is he doing, getting his ashes hauled or falling in love?"

"Love has been known to happen you know."

"Well, fuck that. Let it happen when we don't have a dive party '*who have paid good money*,' ready to go diving."

"Look," Michael says, "why don't you take one of my boys? When D J shows up, I'll shuttle him out there in one of our boats and you can send my guy back at the same time."

"You'd do that?"

"Well sure, why not?"

"By golly, I think that would work. Thank you. But when D J shows up, tell him he's up to his ass in trouble."

Michael chuckled. "Oh, I think he already knows that. But I'll tell him, just to drive the point home."

Michael strode to the lodge to fetch one of his employees that knew about SCUBA. The man he chose for this special mission was named Chester. Chester hurried to his room to gather a few personal items for an overnight trip and hurried to the boat. He smiled broadly as he hopped aboard Siren Song.

"Hello, eberabody. I be Chester. I'm excited to be here. You wan anyting at all, jes let me know."

By now, everyone was aboard the yacht and rearing to go. It only took a minute to cast off lines and bring Siren Song to life. Her big diesel engines thundered, she turned about and carefully weaved her way between the big yachts from Guatemala, out of the marina, then headed across a clear blue sea toward The Great Blue Hole.

Chester indeed knew what he was doing. The first task he set about was checking each of the aluminum 80 scuba tanks to make sure they were fully charged to 3,000 pounds PSI. Then he went from one passenger to another, asking if there was anything they wanted.

Meanwhile, Siren Song was making good way, headed almost directly into the sun. The two large diesel engines droned flawlessly as they pushed the yacht through the clear, blue water. Everyone seemed to be having fun except Maris. She seemed restless. That fact was not lost on either James or Angie, who were both secretly keeping a close eye on her.

Within less than an hour, the coastline of Belize, and Robert's Grove were out of sight. Next stop, Lighthouse Reef and Halfmoon Caye, along the southeast tip of Lighthouse Reef and the closest spit of land to The Great Blue Hole.

Two hours later, very slowly, inching along very carefully, Siren Song navigated her way through the shallow coral along a path that was established long ago by the famous under-sea-explorer, Jacques Cousteau, when he brought the Calypso in through the reef to visit the hole.

That said, this time, the task was made somewhat easier because Captain Gordon Hughes had launched an expensive, high tech drone to fly several hundred feet above the yacht and feed live video footage of precisely where every coral head and encrustation lay. There was no need to peer through the windshield. Every bit of navigational information needed was there, on a full color screen in the console. The Great Blue Hole was reached without incident.

An anchor was secured on the upwind side of the hole, in the shallows which surround the hole. This brought Siren Song to easy rest in thirty feet of water at the very edge of the drop-off. All of the divers looked over the side of the boat into the crystal clear water.

"Wow!" James said. "I can see down all the way to the thermocline."

"I've never seen water this clear," Al said in agreement.

"I had heard this water is so clear that it is almost invisible," Angie said, as she gazed into the depths and stared at the vertical wall of the hole.

"Okay," Gordon Hughes announced. "Everybody look up at the drone and say 'Cheese!'" He had positioned the drone in the perfect angle to capture a group shot of everybody in the stern of the yacht. Everybody looked up and waved happily at the drone and smiled broadly. Once Gordon was satisfied that he had gotten a good picture, he brought the drone in for a landing.

But there is more to see than just the hole. Captain Hughes points at the lighthouse in the distance. "That lighthouse is the reason this reef is named what it is. That little spit of land that the lighthouse is on is called Half Moon Caye, because of its shape. And there has been a lighthouse on it for a couple of hundred years. Actually, the one you see there is relatively new. It's only about a hundred years old. The one before it was destroyed by a hurricane."

Everyone looks at the distant lighthouse and snaps pictures, some with cameras, some with in-phone cameras.

"If you would like, we can go to the caye. It would make a nice side trip before you get serious about your deep dives. You can walk around the whole caye in less than an hour, even if you walk at a casual pace. As for the lighthouse, a curious thing. It used to be on the west side of the caye, but time, tides and wind has moved the whole caye, and now the lighthouse is on the east side."

"Doesn't look like it does much good," Al said.

"What do you mean?"

"Look at that old, wrecked ship there on the edge of the reef. It couldn't be more than a couple of hundred yards from the lighthouse. How far can you see that lighthouse at night, anyway?"

"Oh, probably thirty, maybe forty miles."

"And yet, there the ship is."

"I know. It's not the only one. There are a couple more, farther to the south. We even use one of them as a landmark so we will know where to enter the reef."

"Then why do ships keep crashing against the reef?" Angie asked.

"Well, I don't know about all of them," Gordon said. "But that one closest to the lighthouse involves Caribbean rum. They say the man at the helm was three sheets to the wind. So, it's kind of self-explanatory."

"You leavin' out de bes paht," Chester said.

The way Chester says this entices everyone to turn their attention to him, waiting for more.

"De story go, he had a wo-mahn in de pilot room, trifling wid her. Paying no mind to where he wuz goin'.

"A woman?" Al asks. "They had a passenger aboard a cargo ship?"

"No! Dat de ting. Nobody know where she come from. An after de ship run aground, nobody can find her aboard, anywhere. She vanished."

Scott, as usual, had his camera busy, taking pictures of everything.

"Vanished?" Angie said.

"Yeah, vanished. Jus poof! No mo. No answers. Jus ques-shans." Chester smiles broadly. "Me, I tink it was Minerva."

"Minerva?"

"Minerva de Mermaid. She exists, you know. Nobody can prove it, but dey is a lot of stories."

Angie looks at James. "Evidence?"

James nods his head, yes.

"Yeah, let's go to Halfmoon Caye," Scott says as he checks some images in his camera's window. "It's getting late in the afternoon and I'm hungry. Is there any reason why we can't have a campsite, and a good old-fashioned campfire? A campfire, *and* a cookfire!"

There was a unified cheer that confirmed a consensus of opinion, and so, Siren Song weighed anchor and made her way slowly toward Halfmoon Caye. Once there, the group decided on a picnic spot located not too far from the lighthouse keeper's residence. Within short order, tents, lawn chairs and folding tables were set up, and wood was gathered for a campfire when dark fell. After the long boat ride, everyone was anxious to get sand between their toes for a little while.

After dinner that night, as everyone is sitting around the campfire, relaxing. Ken begins to lay out his plan for the next day. "What I would like to do tomorrow is dive with you around the lagoon right here, adjacent to the caye. That's shallow diving, but there's some really neat stuff to see right out there off the beach less than thirty feet down. This will also help me evaluate your diving abilities before we go deep into the Blue Hole."

"That sounds reasonable," Al Harmon said.

Gordon Hughes is strangely quiet and preoccupied. It is assumed this is because he is still worried about D J.

Seizing the opportunity for a quiet moment with Scott, Angie reaches over, takes his hand and whispers, "Well, if our diving skills are going to be tested tomorrow, maybe we should get in a little swimming practice tonight. That moon looks like it will illuminate the water just enough." She smiles at him, knowingly.

Scott looks at Angie. "Sounds like a paramount idea."

It is a clear star-lit night. The moon has crawled up into the sky like a big lemon pie and illuminates everything in a soft glow. It is the perfect kind of night that lovers crave.

Angie and Scott walk far enough away from the campsite that they can't be seen. They stop at the edge of the picturesque, beautiful lagoon, embrace and let themselves be carried away with a tender, passionate kiss. Scott unhooks Angie's bikini top and drops it onto the sand. She pushes her bikini bottom down and steps out of it, then pushes Scott's bathing suit down to his ankles, where he steps out and flips it on top of Angie's bikini with his toes. Together, hand in hand, they walk into the water to a point where they are in water up to their chests. Anybody watching would have to believe that Angie loved Scott much more than she was willing to let on.

And there is in fact someone watching the two lovers. It is Maris, who is in the shadows, watching, her eyes narrow with green envy. But there is more on her mind. Satisfied that Scott and Angie are otherwise occupied for a while, Maris heads back toward the campsite. Everyone there seems to be enjoying themselves, sitting by the campfire, talking and paying no attention to what anyone not present is doing. This gives Maris the opening she needs to find Scott's camera bag. She silently pads her way to Scott and Angie's tent, goes inside and looks for the camera bag. She spots it, grabs it, opens it and feels around until she finds the camera, then her target, the memory card. Quickly, she extracts it from the camera and zips the bag closed.

Maris now retreats into the dark with the chip until she feels she is far enough away from the campsite. She falls on her knees, then digs a hole in the sand with her hands, while holding the memory card between her lips. When the hole is only six or eight inches deep, she buries the memory card. Thus done, she casually returns to the fireside and the chatter, picks a spot and sits down.

What she doesn't know is that she was being watched by a precocious, suspicious pre-teen. Once Maris is comfortably installed by the fireside, James goes to the place where he saw Maris bury 'something,' digs in the hole until he finds the thing that she was trying to get rid of, the camera's memory card. He tucks the card safely in his bathing suit pocket and returns to the fireside. Maris eyes him, wondering where he has been, but has no idea that he has undone what she tried to do.

───────

Dawn, the next morning: It is just barely that. Inside their tent, Scott snuggles close to Angie in a double sized sleeping bag.

Beautiful singing begins somewhere in the distance. At first it is so soft that it is almost inaudible. But slowly, the volume increases to the point that it rouses Scott from his slumber, and he sits up to listen more carefully, wondering where it is coming from.

Soon, the hypnotic singing entrances him and he works his way out of the sleeping bag, silently, smoothly. Scott steps out the front of the tent completely nude, looks toward the lagoon and sees Maris standing there, waiting for him, her scuba gear in hand. Scott goes to his scuba bag, retrieves his gear and heads for the beach to join Maris. Something is driving him, and nothing seems out of the ordinary about any of this. Maris stands there, smiling. Scott joins her and together they walk into the water.

Underwater, in the lagoon, Scott and Maris swim together among the coral heads, escorted by small fish. The scene is incredibly beautiful and pastoral. Scott and Maris swimming together is so casual, almost like a ballet.

However, this scene is not only unusual, it is impossible, because the music which drew Scott to Maris can still be heard perfectly by him here, underwater. Maris begins to perform a slow-motion dance in front of Scott which is both beautiful and erotic, designed to sexually stimulate Scott. She swoops and swirls, frequently looking at Scott and smiling. Smiling? Yes, she's smiling because she does not have the second stage regulator in her mouth, which she should need to breathe. But for some reason, Scott doesn't connect the dots. Maris not having a regulator doesn't seem out of place at all.

This bewitching underwater performance makes it easy to understand why men have been slaves to the sight and sounds of sirens for hundreds if not thousands of years. Maris now approaches Scott, takes him by the hand and gently pulls him into the dance with her. The dance becomes more and more seductive, but is surprisingly gentle, and although we expect Maris to make her move, she does not.

Her 'move' is to seduce another woman's man and exact revenge on Angie for simply being a woman. She has no power over women, which makes her fear this human woman, as well as resent her because the human, unlike Maris, can love and be loved. Maris secretly watched last night as Angie wrapped her own legs around a man, this man, and had her way with him. Maris is driven to want revenge for that.

Inside the tent, Angie slowly awakens, reaches for Scott and discovering he is not there, she is suddenly wide awake. She sits up and instinctively looks around for him. When she doesn't see him, she quickly pulls on her bikini and pushes her way out of the tent to see if he is beside the campfire. He is not, and then she notices his bathing suit, just inside the flap of the tent. Angie becomes alarmed. She walks over to where Maris had been sleeping without a tent. Maris had said she preferred "under the stars," but in a sleeping bag. Now, Maris is missing.

Angie starts to panic. She decides to quickly get into her dive gear and start a search for him. As she is snapping and strapping on her equipment, she looks up to see James approaching.

"Morning. What's going on?" James asks, unaware of Angie's excited state.

"Scott's missing. So is Maris," Angie says in a tight voice.

"Underwater?"

"That seems to be the most likely place to start looking. Scott's dive gear is gone."

James turns toward Siren Song, which is anchored only yards away, to get his dive gear. "I'll go with you. You definitely should not go alone."

As agile as a gazelle, James runs to Siren Song, pushes up onto the dive platform, climbs the ladder and disappears below deck to retrieve his dive gear. Then, back on deck in the stern of the boat, he screws his regulator onto an aluminum 80, slips a BC onto the tank, gets into it, and climbs back down the ladder in record time. He rejoins Angie, and the two of them walk as fast as they can toward the beach. Suddenly, they pull up short as they look out at the water.

Emerging from the lagoon is Scott and Maris, looking rather spent, and in Scott's case, very guilty. As the two divers walk toward the beach from the water, Scott stops when he sees Angie standing there, watching him. But Maris continues on, walking out of the water, her scuba fins in her hand. She intentionally passes within a couple of feet of Angie and says, "Good morning. Sleep well?"

"Fine, thank you. I see you've had your morning exercise."

"Yes, I have," Maris says coyly. "And it was sooo delightful!"

"Wonderful," Angie says. "Now you've had a sample of

what I get all the time. In fact, you got the leftovers this morning. There couldn't have been very much left.

This quickly erases the smile from Maris' face. The fact that she failed to get Angie's goat does not sit well. It is in extreme contradiction to her plan. Maris stomps off toward the small encampment in a huff.

As she gains distance between herself and Angie, she hears Angie say, "It's good practice for you in case you ever manage to get your own man. I just hope you didn't give mine something he can't get rid of with a shot of penicillin."

Maris makes the mistake of stopping, turning and saying, "What?" Her eyes narrow in anger.

"You heard me," Angie says. "I imagine that thing of yours has been in some pretty filthy places. Matter of fact, I'm wondering, is there anything you haven't fucked, Maris? Don't look now, but there's a distance in your eyes. A distance that makes it impossible for you to ever love anybody, and that makes you a tragic figure. You know, a loser."

Now Maris really is pissed. This is not how things were supposed to turn out at all! Angie, unloading on her like that? Infuriating!

Scott approaches Angie and stops immediately in front of her. "I… I am so sorry. I don't know what came over me. It was weird. I don't know how to explain it."

"Don't worry about it, Lover. I do know how. And I know it wasn't your fault, because there was nothing in the world you could do about it."

"You're not upset?"

"Not with you. And for now, I'm not about to let Twinkle Toes know how I really feel. Come on, let's go somewhere and get some breakfast. I want to bite down on something really hard."

Scott's relief cannot be measured in normal terms. He doesn't understand why 'that' happened to begin with, and he certainly doesn't understand why Angie isn't livid with him.

Angie is a very smart woman. Secretly, she knows that to condemn Scott right now would be the most dangerous thing she could do. If she were to alienate him, even a little bit, Maris would no doubt see this as a breach and use it to get closer to Scott, then kill him. All doubt is removed in Angie's mind about what Maris is. Incredible as it seems, James was right. The bitch is a thousand-year-old siren, morphed as a beautiful woman. And she is here to kill everybody.

CHAPTER TWELVE

Incident in The Grottos

L ater that day, Ken Malloy watches his fledgling divers as well as the seasoned ones from about thirty feet under water as they poke around a beautiful coral reef. James Harmon is buddying with his father. Angie and Scott are buddies. Maris is supposedly buddying with Gordon Hughes, but she is not a good dive buddy. She meanders around, doing her own thing, pretty much ignoring her dive partner. It doesn't matter to Gordon. He isn't sport diving. He's preoccupied with catching lobsters for dinner. The barbequed lobsters at the ranch really whetted his appetite for lobster. And spiny lobsters are the best.

Suddenly, air begins free-flowing from the first stage of James Harmon's regulator, preventing air from reaching the second stage. James cannot breathe. His dad is too far away to try for the auxiliary octopus, so James surfaces. Following protocol, he shows good control, ascending slowly, with his mouth open, exhaling air as he rises to the top. It's only about thirty feet, so it's no big deal. James is a little short of breath by the time he reaches the surface, and he gasps for air, but only for a minute. Then he is fine and starts to swim toward the beach.

At about that same time, Al Harmon manages to capture a huge lobster. He wants to show it to his son, but when he looks around, James isn't there and Al hits the panic button. He retraces his swim path for fifty yards or so. Seeing James nowhere, he takes out his knife and begins banging it against his scuba tank. The noise easily travels to all the divers and they come to Al to see what is wrong.

Meanwhile, Ken Malloy surfaces and sees James walking out of the water onto the beach, while at the same time getting out of his BC. Ken smiles because he knows everything is okay, then he goes back down to where the remaining dive party is and scribbles a note on a small slate he carries for just such an occasion. Everyone reads the note and relaxes, but the upbeat mood of exploration and adventure is destroyed, and everyone heads toward the beach.

Al Harmon wades on shore madder than a hornet and goes to where James is working on his defective regulator. "Goddammit, James! You scared the hell out of us out there."

"But Dad!"

"I don't know how many times I have told you to stay close to your dive buddy when you're diving. So, what do you do? I looked around down there and couldn't find you anywhere."

"I couldn't help it. My regulator went on the blink and I had to surface. I wasn't getting any air."

Al softens, but only slightly. "I'm sorry. But that is still improper procedure. If you would have been close to me, as you were supposed to have been, you could have tapped me on the shoulder and used my octopus. Then we could have surfaced together, *slowly*. You are never supposed to go directly to the surface unless there just is no other choice. Thank God this was a shallow dive. I hate to think what might have happened if we had been down seventy or eighty feet. Did you hold your breath on the way up?"

"Oh hell no. I had my mouth slightly open, and I was exhaling slowly the whole way."

"Well, still, you could have gotten an embolism. Here we are out here in the middle of fucking nowhere, and you could have gotten an embolism."

"If you'd just give me a chance to explain what happened."

"No, I'm going to do the explaining. There are rules, and here is rule number one. If I'm not there, you aren't there. You stay closer to me than a remora to a shark when we're under water. Do you understand that rule?"

"Yessir."

"Alright, this discussion is over." Al turns away and leaves James in tears. Maris, like everyone on the beach, can't help overhearing the dressing down that Al Harmon gave his son. She gets an evil gleam in her eye. It seems that what she heard has provided a solution to a problem for her. That brat kid is the major thorn in her otherwise simple plan. If his father tapes him to his side, problem eliminated!

———

Early evening. The camp on Halfmoon Caye is better established. Chester has organized things, showing that he has done this 'many times' before. There are one or two more tents, more folding chairs and more folding tables.

Most remarkably, the mood is decidedly better. The campfire has been rekindled with fresh wood, but now there is a number three sized washtub sitting on a grill atop the fire. In the washtub is a bubbling caldron of water, beer and spices, and all of that is to cook several large spiny lobsters that have been collected for a sumptuous dinner. Corn on the cob, still in the shucks, cooks in the coals, as well as a couple of breadfruit gathered from a large tree nearby. There is chatter, and laughter. Ken Malloy is telling a story.

"So, the other guy says, 'No, you're wrong. Living on the coast is the perfect training ground for husbands precisely *because* of the hurricanes. That way, the man learns there are just some things with female names that you can't control, so just enjoy the ride.'" This causes mixed laughter.

Then Chester makes the announcement that his nose informs him it is time to remove the lobsters from the pot. He grabs large tongs and a platter. As he removes the beautiful lobsters from the boiling water, there are 'Oohs and Ahs' and comments about 'Can't wait.' The corn on the cob is removed from the ashes and shucked, and the breadfruit, which has also been cooking in the coals, is raked out, placed in a bowl and cut open. Angie is the first to try a piece.

"Wow!" she says. "This really does taste like fresh baked bread. Who knew?"

"Well, here's a bit of history for you," Ken says, because Ken loves to tell a story. "The breadfruit trees in this area are the result of Captain William Bligh's second trip to Tahiti in the early 1790s. Bligh actually made it to Tahiti, gathered the breadfruit plants, and then delivered his cargo to Jamaica safely on his second try. They planted the breadfruit trees, which took the transplant very well, and the trees grew. But after all that trouble, the people they planned on feeding with the breadfruit didn't like it and wouldn't eat it."

"Who were they planning on feeding it to?" Scott asked.

"Slaves that worked on the plantations. They had never seen breadfruit before. Wasn't part of their diet, and they wanted nothing to do with it. Be that as it may, over the years, breadfruit trees managed to find their way onto almost every island in the Caribbean, plus the mainland, from Guatemala, to Belize and especially Honduras. The fruit is actually pretty good, and as you can see, the trees are beautiful. Big, with large leaves. Perfect for shade. Paul Gaugin used them in a lot of his paintings."

By now, everyone was digging into the lobsters. Most of the responses were 'oh my goodness!' as everyone stuffed their faces with delicious food. There was also beer or wine to compliment the meal.

It was an 'almost miracle' end to a day that started out as tense as a snail crawling along a razor blade. To that end, Maris, although present, was quiet and withdrawn. She was confused by the behavior of these humans. They rebounded so quickly, so easily from any kind of adversity.

Al, sitting next to James, turned to his son and said softly, "I'm sorry I blew up today, son. It just scared the hell out of me when I looked around and you weren't there. And I'm just nervous anyway, for some reason. I don't know why. Can you forgive your old man?"

James reaches out enough to hug his father with one arm. "Sure dad. I understand. Besides, I guess I really did screw up. I won't do it again. But right now, I want some more melted butter! I mean, there *are* priorities here!"

Al Harmon's face lights up, and he laughs. "Melted butter, coming up!"

Chester hears the request. "Melted buttah? I jus happen to have plenty, right heah." Chester retrieves a small, black cast iron pot that is sitting to one side of the grill and brings it to James and Al. "You want some too, sah?"

"Sure, why not. Thank you," Al says.

The dinner progresses with lots of happy chatter and a cool breeze coming in off the water. More than one of the adults has a wee too much to drink. This includes the group's dive master, Ken Malloy, who is obviously feeling the glow of good food and friendship. He pushes his chair back and stands, with his wine glass in his hand.

"Alright! Here ye hear ye! I want to make a toast, and at this point I am just about toasted enough to do that!" There is laughter all around the table with comments.

"I just want to say that after watering all of you... Oops! I mean, 'watching' all of you, polliwog around the lagoon today, I feel very confident about taking you, *all* of you, into the Great Blue Hole tomorrow. Just as soon, that is, that I get over my hangover, which is bound to be a doozie!"

Laughter.

"No, I am quite serious. All of you, including James H there, have demonstrated good instincts, and natural diving abilities, some of which just can't be taught. Either you have them, or you don't. And you good people clearly do have them. So, to you I say, 'Salud, dinero, amor y tiempo para gosar los!' Which, by the way, doesn't have a damn thing to do with diving, but it's a fine toast." Everybody laughs and joins Ken as he hoists his glass, then drinks.

Then Scott, who is about half plowed by now, stands up,

wine glass in hand and says, "Some Come Up Barely Alive!"

"Here, here!" Gordon says, and everybody drinks that toast.

It is a good thing nobody is watching Maris. They would see the evil leer on her face, a look of envy that even she does not understand. She has never known jealousy before and does not know how to deal with it. She wants to lash out. But who would she lash out at first? She is envious of every person here for one reason or another. Her frustration is immeasurable.

The party pushes back the night. Somebody piles a bunch of wood on the campfire, making it warm and welcoming, and bright. Ken turns up his boom box. This spit of land is too far out at sea to pick up any decent radio stations, so Ken has had enough foresight to bring along some very good CDs, including one in particular which seems to fit the exotic mood of this location. It is called, "Olias of Sunhillo," by Jon Anderson and the music is very exotic sounding.

Indeed, Maris herself seems entranced by the sounds and has begun to dance around the fire. Almost everybody is too much in the bag to pay very much attention to Maris' movements. All that is except James and Angie, whose vigil has not relaxed. They look at one another as Maris dips and swirls in a circle around the fire. Her movements are somehow very primitive, very ancient, very Greek. Not in a way that can be described in words, but the inference is there. This, it seems, is the first moment when Maris has actually let her guard down. She is entranced, lost in the music. Is this the siren's Achille's Heel? She uses music as a weapon. But can it also be her Trojan Horse? She is, after all, vulnerable. It is the closest thing she has revealed about herself to showing real feelings.

———

It is an hour past dawn. The Caribbean sky is clear as a bell. The pinks of the morning sun have faded to light blue. Birds are aloft, floating on the soft sea breeze air currents. Particularly frigate birds, with their scissor tails, floating weightlessly a hundred feet up, looking for breakfast.

Siren Song inches her way back through Lighthouse Reef toward the Great Blue Hole. Again, the drone is far overhead, helping with navigation. Every asset must be brought to bear, because if Siren Song were to hit a coral head, even at a slow speed, the trip would be over. The Zodiak inflatable lifeboat, being pulled behind Siren Song on a tethered line is a constant reminder to be careful.

In addition to everything else, Ken Malloy stands at the tip of the bow pulpit, looking down into the clear water, ready to warn Captain Hughes of any obstacle that radar, underwater bow cameras, or the drone might miss.

Although it is an impeccably beautiful, flawless morning, something is in the air that makes everybody want to take extra precautions. Most people aboard Siren Song assume it is because they are about to embark on a very deep and somewhat dangerous dive. Angie Holland and James Harmon have their own secret reasons for apprehension. If their theory is right, they are going to dive straight into the siren's lair. She might decide now is the time to strike in order to make her point. They must be ready.

Angie pulls James to the side in the far stern of the boat.

"I don't understand. Why don't we just shoot the bitch and be done with it?"

James sighed. "And you were the one who wanted to be careful to 'make sure' before we did anything."

"Okay, that's true. But now I am sure. I'm very sure. That fucking trollop is a siren."

"You're just mad because she dinged Scott. That isn't evidence."

Angie looks at James and blinks. "It is as far as I'm concerned!"

"Believe me, I'm with you. I would l *love* to just shoot her right in the brisket and be done with it. But if there is even the tiniest chance that we're wrong about who she is, that would be murder. I'm too young to be somebody's bitch in prison."

"Christ-o-mity, James! How do you know about such things?"

"This is the age of information, Ang. I read a lot. Besides, practically nothing is taboo on TV these days. You know, my dad told me about old TV shows where married couples couldn't even be seen together in the same bed. They had to use twin beds for scenes."

"Yeah, that's true...so I've heard!" Angie smiles a momentary smile.

"All we can do is watch her closely," James says. "At the very first sign of treachery, that she is going to try something hinky, we'll pounce on her."

Angie looks to where Scott is standing on the stern to one side, shooting pictures of almost everything they see. "Just watch her close," Angie says. "In my opinion, she is the personification of evil. As pure an evil as evil gets."

"You're right," James says. "What makes it worse is that

she's on a mission. That's not like being on a rant or something. What she has planned is premeditated, calculated mayhem. If she had it her way, she would be the only one left standing when this thing is over."

"And that day just might be today."

James nods yes, that he agrees and understands.

Inside, at the console, Captain Hughes stares intently, but confidently at the instruments in front of him including the live video footage being sent from overhead by the drone. "Get ready, everybody," Gordon says.

Suddenly, the marine radio comes to life. It is Michael from Robert's Grove Lodge calling. Captain Hughes picks up his microphone and speaks into it. "This is Siren Song. How you doing this morning, Michael?"

"Good, mahn, good! How are things on Lighthouse reef?"

"So far, so good. But the day is young!" Gordon says in light humor. "Had a nice night or two of Halfmoon Caye. More delicious lobsters, and we cooked some breadfruit!"

"Ah, breadfruit. I love it. Down here, we call it 'mazapan'. I like it cooked several different ways. So, what's on today's agenda?"

"At this moment, I'm moving Siren Song into position over The Blue Hole, preparing for the first deep dive."

"That's great. Tell everyone to be extra careful. Well, I still don't have any news for you, good or bad, about D J. I'm beginning to get a little worried."

"You aren't the only one. He's never pulled a boner like this before. I mean, he's disappeared once or twice for a few hours, and then showed up with a monster of a hangover, swearing to never do it again. But never like this. I think he may have gotten himself in some real trouble this time."

"Let's hope not. I'm no giving up yet."

"I appreciate that. Have you checked the cop-shop?"

"Yah, mahn. Checked the hospital too. I called the police in Belize City. Nothing. Nobody has even seen him. It's like he has just vanished."

"Damn! Something tells me, that young-un has managed to go and really get his tail in a twist, this time." Captain Hughes said into the microphone. "Okay Michael, thanks, and let me know the minute you learn anything, please."

"No prob-lem," Michael said in his thick Belizian accent.

"Something is fucked up about this trip," Gordon Hughes says more to himself than anybody. "I can't put my finger on it. But I've felt it since we pulled out of port in San Leon."

Just at that moment, Siren Song clears the last coral head and enters the environs of Great Blue Hole. Captain Hughes looks for the upwind side, steers the boat there and asks Ken Malloy, already on the bow, if he would throw the anchor into a safe spot. This done, the main motors are shut down on the yacht and Ken Malloy gathered all the divers around for a pre-dive briefing.

James turned to Angie in the stern of the boat and said quietly, "Why do I feel like I'm going to the OK Corral?"

Angie silently looked at James. James said, just as quietly, "I have a plan that I need your help with."

"Name it," she said.

"You see that silver-colored aluminum 80 over there that has a small check mark on it?"

Angie looked at the tanks, found the right one and nodded.

"I've let all the air out of that puppy except for about

one hundred pounds psi. I've noticed that Maris never checks her pressure gauge to see how much air she's got. Never checks her regulator either. All she goes by is the color of her BC. Watch when we gear up and switch her regulator and BC to that tank. Better yet, put my defective regulator on it. By the time we get down to150 feet, she should run out of air. If she doesn't panic, we've got her. Conclusive proof that she isn't getting her air from the tank at all."

Angie smiled, "James, that's genius. But you're going to have to distract her, somehow, while I make the switch."

"Yeah. I'll think of something. It's going to have to be something that draws everybody, not just her."

"When?"

"When Ken finishes his briefing. Oh! There's something else I've been meaning to tell you about."

"What?"

"The night you and Scott went skinny dipping in the lagoon."

"Yeah, what about it?"

"I saw her take the memory card out of Scott's camera and bury it. I was watching the whole time. She didn't see me, so I went and dug it up. I've still got it."

"Why would she want to do a thing like that?"

"Well, you know how some people look at Maris and think she's a blond, others think she's a brunette? Some people think she a teenager. Other people think she's in her thirties? My guess is, the image we see from that memory card will show the true Maris, and she would be exposed in more than one way."

"Give me the card."

James pulls the card from his bathing suit pocket and hands it to Angie. "What are you going to do?"

"Put it in Gordon's computer the first chance I have and bring up any image with her in it. I really want to see what that minx looks like."

But there was no time to do any of that. Ken Malloy called the divers together for a final pre-dive check. Everyone found places to sit or stand in the stern of the boat, so they could clearly hear their dive-master. Scott stood next to Ken.

"Diving the Great Blue Hole is one of the most exotic dives undertaken by sport divers. It's not a dive where you see great colorful fish or really neat coral, although the coral surrounding the Great Blue Hole pretty well makes up for that. What you're going to experience down there is a sandy slope that runs down at about a thirty-degree angle down from a few feet to about thirty feet. And then there is a sheer drop off that just plummets and keeps going straight down. Because of the clarity of the water, some people get a little bit of a start when they go from the sandy slope, over the edge to the drop off. They feel like they're falling.

"As you all know, this is a very deep dive. And the destination is, of course, those grottos. The ceiling of them begins at about 120 feet. The opening is about thirty feet, so the bottom of the grottos is at about one hundred and fifty feet, more or less.

"Because of the depth, many people start to feel uneasy. In 1990, we had one woman who really got a bad case of raptures. She started hallucinating. She was inside one of the grottos, which was lucky for her. She panicked and started trying to swim straight up. Luckily, she hit the ceiling of the grotto. This gave my assistant and I time to grab her by her arms, then try to calm her and slowly bring her out of the grotto so we could swim to the surface.

"If she had gone off out in front of the grottos where there was nothing to slow her down, she would be dead. Now, I'm telling you this story for a reason. My point is, if you begin to feel uneasy, or even a little bit panicky, or if you start to hallucinate, use your knife to tap on your tank and Scott or I will come to you. If you feel like you want to surface, point up and one of us will accompany you. Don't take chances. Absolute bottom time is thirty minutes, and that is from the time you leave the surface. Even so, I would feel a lot better if you would cut yourself five. This is a deep dive. Make no mistake, it is a dangerous dive."

Scott stepped forward and added to the briefing. "We will be dropping several tanks over the side, equipped with octopuses, secured to ropes. These tanks will be suspended at the ten- and twenty-foot levels. There will also be dive tables tied to them. Follow your J card closely. Make those decompression stops. We don't need any cases of the bends out here. We're here to have a good time, not film a segment for a TV survival show. We'll be watching bottom time very closely. When Ken or I rap on our tank signaling that it is time to come up, do not hesitate for a second. I don't care if you think you've found the lost treasure of the Caribbean. Start your trip up immediately when signaled."

Everybody chuckled, but they got the message. Have fun but play it safe. Maris' body language revealed that she thought the briefing was a waste of time. She planned on murdering everybody anyway. So, what difference did it make how they died?

This was a fact that was not overlooked by Angie. Just then, a couple of large hammerhead sharks between fifteen and twenty feet in length, casually swam beneath the boat. An alert went up from Al Harmon. "Damn! Look at those sharks." And this provided the distraction that Angie needed to switch Maris' BC and also to hook up the defective regulator.

When she was finished, she quickly joined everybody else at the gunwale of the boat, looking at the sharks. "Oh shit!" Angie said. "I really don't like sharks. And I've heard about these fucking hammerheads in the Blue Hole. James, can I ask a big–big favor?"

"Sure. What's that?"

"Can I borrow your shark stick for this first dive?"

"Sure," James said. "Let me load it."

"Stick?" Maris asked, when she overheard the exchange.

"Bang stick," Angie said, looking straight at Maris. "It's also called a thumper. Also, a shark stick."

"What's it for?" Maris asked.

"To kill sharks. I don't like sharks. If one of them gets anywhere near me, I will blow his frigging brains all over the Caribbean, compliments of James' 'shark stick'."

Maris looks horrified. "I can't believe you'd do that! Sharks won't bother you."

"Really?" Angie said. "Maybe they won't bother you. Maybe you have some special kind of relationship with them, but I don't. And I don't want one. Anything that threatens me is going to get it, one way or the other. And I mean, *anything*!"

Angie never takes her eyes off of Maris as she delivers this short speech. And when she finishes, she looks at Maris and smiles knowingly. There is fear in Maris' eyes that she cannot hide. Just then, James appears from below deck with the bang stick.

"Just please be careful where you point that horrible thing," Maris says nervously.

"Oh, don't worry," Angie says with a smile. "I won't point it at anything that I don't intend to kill."

And now, Maris' eyes flash as she dismisses Angie with a final, dismissive look.

Angie looks at James as if to say, 'Got the bitch!'

Everybody gears up. They have already attached their BC and regulator to filled scuba tanks. James watches Maris because he is nervous that she might notice the regulator switch and/or the low air pressure in the tank. But she is so furious at Angie that Maris notices nothing. She slips her BC on and latches the catch.

Interesting, James thinks to himself. *Divers are usually intimately knowledgeable of their equipment. Maris doesn't seem to give a shit. Makes you wonder if the gear is really hers?*

As dive master, Ken Malloy is the first one off the stern dive platform of Siren Song, into the water. From a position near the boat, he can watch the rest of his divers as each person enters the water. When all divers are in the water, Ken gives the hand signal reminding everybody that they are to stay close together. When they give a thumbs up, Ken responds in kind, then turns his hand over, pointing his thumb downward, which is the signal to dive. Hands go in the air with the purge valve on each BC, letting the air escape. When each BC is deflated, the diver turns downward and dives.

The divers cluster about twenty feet down, doing a final check of their gear to see if everything is working alright. Then, Ken Malloy leads the way toward the drop-off which is The Great Blue Hole.

Over the edge they go, now in a slow-motion free fall. As they sink deeper and deeper, the divers are impressed that The Great Blue Hole is everything they have heard it was. The water is crystal clear, so clear that it seems it would be incapable of buoying a human body. So, there was a little tightening of the gut when the divers went over the edge of the slope and began the plummet straight down. As they descend deeper and deeper, they each grab at their nose guard on the dive mask to constantly blow and equalize inner ear pressure.

This is the barren wall that Scott saw in his dream. He had seen it previously, but now the stark reality of it is confusing. Did his dream remind him of the wall? Or does the wall remind him of his dream? Either way, it borders on the supernatural.

There are only a few small fish to be seen as the divers descend, deeper and deeper. At about eighty feet, the divers encounter a thermocline. It is a milky white layer in the water, about ten feet thick and spreads out for a thousand feet, all the way across the hole like a milky lid. They cannot see anything below it. All they know is, to get to where they want to go, they must swim down, through it. Since they have been told about the thermocline, it only represents a minimal threat and they hesitate only a moment, then allow themselves to disappear in the milk, but only for a moment. Then it is above them. Here, beneath the thermocline, the water is decidedly cooler.

That isn't all. Perhaps because of the milky veil, the aura here is spooky. The ambient light is about half what it was above the thermocline. It is diffused, shadowy, and by now, nitrogen narcosis is beginning to get a grip on the divers. In a way, it's similar to eating peyote. All the colors and all of the shadows are enhanced or appear to be something other than what they are, mere shadows.

One of the most impressive things about here, and this depth is the stillness. Nothing moves. Everything is like in a still-shot photograph. The divers look all around them as they descend, deeper and deeper, impressed with what they are seeing and trying to believe that it is real.

And then all of a sudden, there they are! The grottos. Up close, right in front of them, so close. So very close! And so very ominous looking!

The divers are 120 feet underwater. Martini's law has a grip on all of them. Imagination mixes with nitrogen at this depth to create a frightening aspect. The grottos look like the inside of a giant moray eel's mouth, with jagged teeth on both the top and bottom jaw, making a terrible, dangerous narrow passageway between them.

In reality, they are large mineral formations, stalactites and stalagmites formed millions of years ago, when this island was above water. When the water level rose following the last ice age, the mineral formations remained because of their limestone base structure. Time changed them very little, except to make them appear more ominous by coating them with sediment. Their dominating, huge appearance is definitely impressing the divers. One tell-tale sign is the volume of bubbles being exhaled from the divers' regulators.

Scott positions Angie beside one of the huge mineral formations, for scale, and takes her picture. He then gives her a thumb to index finger signal, confirming that he got a good photo.

James is being a good son and diver and staying close to his father, though he stops frequently to stare in awe at the giant mineral formations. Ken Malloy swims out away from the wall several feet so that he can see at a wide angle and make sure he keeps an eye on all of his divers.

Suddenly, the regulator Maris is using begins to spew air from the first stage which is attached to the nozzle of the aluminum 80 scuba tank. James sees this, and so does Angie. The one person who didn't seem to notice at all is Maris, and under normal circumstances, she would have been the one affected. No air would have been able to reach the 2nd stage of her regulator, which contains the mouthpiece and is the part a diver breathes from. She should have been rushing to the diver nearest her and grabbing that person's octopus, so she could breathe. But she did not. She apparently didn't even notice the breach.

Her failure to do so confirms everything James and Angie suspect about her. Maris is a water breathing, creature of the sea. Maris is a siren!

Maris continues to swim very casually, unshaken by her escaping stream of air bubbles. She polliwogs, although she does not enter the grottos. It seems so obvious that she has been here before.

Al Harmon also starts to swim deeper into the grottos. James watches his father, but chooses to hang back a little, reluctant to enter into such a dark area where visibility is limited. Everything is calm. The only sound is that of exhaled bubbles from various regulators, and the sight of an occasional flash as Scott takes copious pictures. All is peaceful.

As Al Harmon swims deeper into the grotto, he maneuvers around the side of a very large stalactite when suddenly, something very large and tremendously powerful lashes out at him. Whatever it is, the aim is slightly off, and 'it' hits Al hard, against his right shoulder.

The impact knocks Al's mask off. It also knocks his regulator out of his mouth, which falls back over his right shoulder. This wouldn't normally be a problem. Any diver can simply reach back to the tank valve, get a grip on the regulator hose and pull the regulator back in place. But the crushing blow from the attack may have dislocated Al's shoulder. Now, with the searing pain of the wound, Al grapples with his shoulder, exhales his air and begins sinking.

The man's death is almost certain. Or would be. The pain is so intense that he is close to blacking out. But then, with lightning speed and exceptional strength for someone twelve years old, James Harmon rushes forward and grabs his father's BC by the backpack, retrieves the regulator and puts it in his father's mouth. Then he begins to back pedal out of the grotto, pulling his father with him, using the backpack on the BC as a handle.

Al coughs a couple of times and breathes hard for a minute, but he is okay. Ken arrives to help. James hands off the BC to Ken for a minute, then swims to the floor of the grotto to retrieve his father's face mask. He rushes to his father with the mask and slips the strap over his father's head, then fitting the mask in place. Al is able to use his left hand to press the top of the mask to his forehead and exhale into the mask, thus purging the water from it, so he can see. He nods his head, indicating all is well.

James takes a position on the right side of his father. Ken Malloy takes the left side. With his free hand, Ken Malloy starts banging on his scuba tank with his knife, the signal to abandon whatever any of the divers are doing and start the slow assent to the top. The divers are ready to go in any case. They have seen that Al Harmon is in distress. And even though they don't know what has happened, their training has taught them that when one diver is in trouble, all divers leave together. They gather close around Al, James and their dive master. Scott takes a picture of this scene as they ascend.

James looks around, trying to spot Maris, trying to figure out if she had anything to do with this. But she has apparently violated the rules of scuba diving and gone wandering off on her on. She swims at them from at least a hundred feet away. For her to have had anything to do with this, she would have to be able to swim at an incredible speed, even for a siren. As she approaches, she stares back at him. But he cannot tell what is in her eyes. Still, he cannot take his eyes off of her as they head toward the surface. She sees James staring at her and finally cannot maintain her gaze any longer. She intentionally looks away, toward the surface. She still has not noticed that her regulator has malfunctioned.

Angie's look says it all. She wants to kill Maris. It seems like it is all Angie can do to restrain herself and keep from charging forward with the bang stick to dispatch the siren.

The ascent is intentionally slow. Ken Malloy has to constantly adjust his BC as well as Al Harmon's BC in an effort to guard the integrity of the slow rise to the surface. Any diver knows that to "go up too fast" is a death sentence. Air embolisms are the number one killer of divers.

What causes an embolism? Air bubbles, trapped in the lungs for any reason grow larger as the body ascends. Expanding air bubbles rupture the alveoli (tiny air sacs) in the lungs, allowing air bubbles to enter directly into the blood stream. Those bubbles travel to the brain and, it's all over, Charley!

When the divers enter the thermocline, James takes a position in front of his father, holding his dad's BC by the front, checking on all sides, guarding against a surprise attack by anything...or anyone.

Above the thermocline, while no one is watching her, Maris' eyes roll back in her head and she emits a short, strange, high frequency noise. Suddenly, two hundred yards away, four hammerhead sharks, schooling together, have heard the noise made by the siren, and they immediately become agitated. They respond by turning toward the source off the sound, and begin swimming, closing in on the divers.

At the twenty feet decompression stop, Al is trying hard to hang on. He is in extreme pain. James sees this and squeezes his father's left hand in an effort to say, "Hang in there. We'll be on the boat in short order."

The hammerhead sharks have now arrived in close proximity to the divers, and sensing something in the water not unlike a wounded fish in distress, they start circling a little too closely to the dive party. Angie, who has been carrying the bang stick, and is already tense because of Al's unexplained injury, watches as the sharks circle closer and closer.

When one shark gets too close, she takes the bang stick off safety, swims at it, presses the bang stick against the shark's head and pushes hard. There is a loud explosion. Immediately, there is a cloud of blood, carnage and gore around the shark's head as the animal writhes in death throes and begins to sink out of sight into the depths of the Great Blue Hole. The dispatched shark is suddenly attacked by the other three sharks in a feeding frenzy, which distracts them from the dive party.

Angie watches as the animal retreats in death, being torn apart by other sharks that a moment ago were its companions. She then looks at Maris and sees Maris' eyes are huge with stark terror. Angie takes undisguised pleasure in this. It is reassuring to her to know that the siren can experience fear. She looks over at James, who is still assisting his father. Luckily, he is returning her gaze. She winks at him.

A couple of minutes later, the divers have outgassed the required amount of time and can continue their ascent to the surface. James and Ken help Al Harmon onto the dive platform, then Chester is there and joins them in helping the injured man up the ladder to the stern of Siren Song.

Al struggles into the nearest chair where Chester, James and Ken Malloy help him get out of his dive gear. His wound is severe and excruciatingly painful. Still, he mumbles, "Don't let this end the dive... I mean the trip."

CHAPTER THIRTEEN

Let's Cut Our Losses

Gordon is there, sees there has been an accident and grabs for Siren Song's first aid kit. He rushes to the stern to help the victim but isn't sure what the accident is. Once Al is seated as comfortably as possible in his chair, Ken Malloy flops down in a chair beside him and asks, "What happened down there?"

"I really don't know," Al says, his voice revealing his pain. "I was polliwogging real slow around the head of this big stalactite when something struck out from behind it and hit me like a truck."

"You didn't see what it was?"

"Moved too fast. It came out, hit me in one move, and then it was gone. If it wasn't for the angle, I might think it was a piece of falling mineral formation. It was that solid. All I know is, I saw stars when it hit me."

"That wasn't stars," Scott Carrington said. It was my flash. I was taking a picture not too far from you when whatever it was clobbered you. I might have gotten the whole thing on memory card. Have to check and see."

Maris, overhearing this, suddenly looks worried, but tries to hide it. Angie sees Maris worried expression and grabs Scott's hand.

"Give me the memory card." Angie says, loud enough for Maris to hear.

Scott looks at Angie, standing next to him. "What?"

"Give me the card, *right now*."

Scott retrieves his camera from where he has laid it on the deck. While he is removing it from the water-proof case, Ken turns to Al. "We've got a man in pain here. I've got to get you out of this wet suit."

"I don't think there's going to be but one way to do that," Al says.

"Yeah, that's what I was afraid of. But I hate having to ruin such an expensive wet suit."

"Fuck that. Don't give it a thought. You've got to do what you've got to do. I don't imagine I'll be doing much more diving the rest of this trip anyway. But I'll bet I know what to do with that bottle of J D pain killer below deck."

"After this dive, I might be giving you some help," Ken said as he pulled out his knife and began to carefully cut away the top of Al Harmon's wet suit. "I don't understand," Ken adds. "We have been down in that hole on about a dozen trips, made at least two deep dives per trip, and never has anything like this happened, ever! We've never even seen anything down there big enough to inflict this kind of an attack." Ken Malloy shakes his head in disbelief.

Al looks up at James, who is standing close beside his father. "I don't think I want to go another second without telling my son how grateful I am, and how incredibly proud I am of him. James, I've never seen anything like what you did down there. You're twelve years old, but you, my boy, are not a boy. You are a man, and a damn fine one!"

"I'd have to agree, one hundred percent," Ken Malloy said. Then everyone else chimed in and agreed.

Ken reaches a place under the armpit that is hard to cut with his knife and he doesn't want to take a chance on cutting Al. "You got any scissors on this old scow?" he asks Gordon.

"Hey! Watch out whose tub you're calling a scow," Gordon teases. "Yeah, I might have some scissors somewhere." Gordon turns and goes inside the salon, closing the door behind him.

Everyone chuckles, albeit it is a nervous chuckle. At least it helps to relieve some of the tension, a little bit.

Maris looks at the divers and is non-plussed. Her expression says, 'these humans are more resilient than I thought'.

"You people are amazing," Maris finds herself saying, involuntarily. "A person almost died down there. Then we were assaulted by sharks. Now, here you are, sitting on the boat, smiling and happy, and joking around."

Angie is not about to let this opportunity for a little dig pass by. Oh no!

"You ought to try getting to really know people sometime, Sweetie. Who knows, you might like them!"

Strangely, there is no anger in Maris' eyes as a result of Angie's verbal poke. Instead, she looks away, and seems slightly sad. This because she knows inside that she can never 'be' one of them. She is alone. Eternally alone. And like it or not, the end of her kind is coming. There is no way to stop it.

A couple of minutes later, Gordon has returned with

scissors, and Ken has managed to cut the top of the wet suit off of Al. It lies in pieces on the stern deck. Gordon has done his best to inspect the wound, and Al Harmon is now lying down, prone, on his back, in the stern of the boat, atop a large beach towel. Gordon Hughes sits in a chair beside him.

"From what I can tell, nothing is broken," Gordon says. "But that shoulder is badly dislocated, and the muscle is bruised all to hell. We're gonna have to try to pop that arm back in place or you are gonna be one miserable sum-bitch till we can get you out of here and to a hospital in Belize."

"Where's that bottle of pain killer?" Al pleads. "I think if I take a snort of that, it will help with pre-op here."

"You've got a point," Ken says, and goes into the salon to fetch the bottle of J D. He returns quickly, unscrews the top and hands the bottle to Al. Al takes the bottle with his left hand, puts it to his mouth and drinks deeply, then hands the bottle back to Ken.

"Wait a damn minute," Gordon says. "I think I need a good pull on that bottle for a little added courage myself. What I'm about to do hurts me as bad as it does 'the patient.'"

Without a word, Ken hands the bottle to Gordon, who also takes a pretty good swig, then hands the bottle back to Ken.

Ken looks at the bottle. "Well, what the hell. Why should I be the only one on the boat who is 'serfically pober'?" Then Ken turns the bottle up and drinks. When he's finished, he says, "Okay, Doctor Hughes, I think the O R is all ready now."

"Here, let me hold that bottle for you," Angie says as

she reaches for the J D. Then she follows the men's example by turning the bottle up and taking a deep swig.

Sea birds have begun to gather around the boat, finding perch spots on coral heads that are protruding above the water. They are alert, always waiting for some kind of edibles to be jettisoned. So, they are witness to the sound of agony when Captain Gordon Hughes firmly takes Al Harmon's wrist, places one foot beneath Al's arm pit and yanks hard.

"Ohhhh! Shit! Mother Theresa Gonzalez, shit, shit, shit. Oh, mother fucker that hurt! Hand me that pain killer again. I need a *lot* of frigging pain killer!"

"Sorry," Gordon Hughes said. "But I think I got the arm back in the socket. That doesn't mean it's gonna hurt much less, but at least it can start healing."

"Oh no. Don't apologize," Al says. "You did a great job and I appreciate the treatment. I just hope I *survive* the operation. You've heard the old joke; the operation was a success, but the patient died."

Gordon chuckles. "You'll survive. Just keep on taking regular doses of that pain killer and I assure you, you'll be feeling no pain at all in no time."

Al Harmon holds his shoulder with his left hand. Then turns to look at James. "My apologies for using that kind of language in front of you, Son."

"What kind of fucking language are you talking about?" James says very nonchalantly, with a smile.

———

It is night. Everyone is gathered around in the salon of Siren Song. Al Harmon is propped up on the sofa, with ample pillows positioned in strategic places around the shoulder. His arm is now in a sling.

Angie and James sit on the carpeted floor, playing a card game. Maris is sitting in a chair, but she seems strangely withdrawn, and looks out the window into the darkness, not really participating in any of the comradery taking place around her.

Everyone, except for James and possibly Maris is a little drunk by now. The others all nurse drinks as they talk.

"Something else is bothering me," Ken says. "I've been in the Blue Hole a bunch of times. I've seen those same damn sharks several times. But I've never seen them act up the way they did today. Weird! Wonder why they had a bug up their ass?"

"Strange, very strange," Angie says, as she looks at her cards. "Gin!" she says.

"Already?" James complains.

"I just can't figure what got 'em stirred up?" Ken says. "You know, I had reservations about James bringing that bang stick on this trip. But I've got to tell you, now I'm glad he did. Better to have shark sushi than one of us wind up another victim."

"Ain't that the gospel?" Al says three sheets to the wind now from the J D 'pain killer'.

Gordon is bothered by something. Finally, he says, "Uh, may I have everybody's attention. I need to say something." Gordon pauses a minute. "I think I have had enough of Al's pain killer by now, that I can get this out. Now, first of all, I want to make it perfectly clear, what I am about to say is no reflection on any of you. I mean that from the bottom of my heart. You are all delightful people, and from what I can gather, excellent scuba divers, and

you've all got your ducks in a row. However. That said...
well, here it is..."

"Ohhh, this isn't going to be good!" Al Harmon says,
jokingly.

"I'm afraid you're right," Gordon says. "But damn the
torpedoes, full speed ahead! People, friends, we should have
never begun this excursion. I have felt, since the day we
pulled out of port in San Leon that something was wrong,
something was afoul. I can't put my finger on exactly what
it is, but *something* is out of place. Now, we've had one man
go missing. He still hasn't turned up. They pulled one
floater out of the harbor and thought that might be him, but
damage to the body suggested that person had been in the
water for quite a while, certainly a lot longer than D J had
been missing."

"What kind of 'damage to the body'?" Angie asks,
slightly alarmed.

"Uh, I'm not sure specifically. Michal said the crabs had
been eating on it. Most of the flesh on the head was eaten
away. Not a pretty picture, for sure. Anyway, as captain of
this vessel, it is my responsibility to keep all of you safe. It
is with that in mind that I have made the decision to turn
back to Belize at dawn. We're going back, directly to Belize
City, where all of you will disembark and a limo will deliver
you to the casino hotel there. In your case, Al, directly to the
hospital E R. I will pay all expenses. I will also refund your
charges and fees for his trip. I ask you to please not be
disappointed, or for that matter, mad, but rather, try to
understand my position.

"Now, '*if*' you decide you want to try again at another
time, you might be able to do that, but with another
Captain. I have decided to sell Siren Song to Michael at

Robert's Grove Resort and retire. When a man starts to feel like I am feeling at this minute, it's time to pull the plug and get the hell out. I thank the Lord above that I have enough wisdom left in me to recognize that. So... Thank you for listening to me. This hasn't been easy to say. But a wise man knows when to cut his losses and walk off the stage."

"Wow!" Ken says. Well, I'm as surprised as anyone. But I respect the Captain's position. I think he has our safety and comfort and best interests at heart. And, if I were him, I'd have to say that today's little incident at one hundred and fifty feet was the last straw too. So, let me be the first to say, I respect your decision, Captain. Let me shake your hand." Ken extends his hand to Captain Hughes.

"Thank you, Ken," Captain Hughes says.

"Well," Angie says, as she stands up. "To be perfectly honest with you, this place gives me the creeps. It sounded bizarre in Scott's dream when he told me about it. I have never been to the Great Blue Hole before. And now, seeing it for real has certainly lived up to that dream. I'm more than ready to get the hell out of here."

She stands up and places her hand lovingly on Scott's shoulder. "What say, Lover. You ready to go home?"

Scott thinks it over for a minute. "Yeah, I agree. It's time to go home. To be honest, I don't think I ever want to come back here. I've been here before, but this time was a bummer. Hopefully, I got enough good pictures to make the trip worthwhile. But yeah, sayonara!"

Ken turns to Al. "You're not going to get any argument out of me," Al says, then takes another sip of his drink.

Ken turns to Maris. "Maris?

Maris never stops looking out the window. "Whatever

everyone wants to do. I don't care." Her voice is now soft, resigned.

"Okay, not that it was up for a vote, but it's nice to know that we're all in agreement," Ken says. At least we got you all certified and you did your check-out dives. I'm sorry the Great Blue Hole was a disappointment. But you know what? Gordon is right. There has been 'something' off center about this trip from the get-go. I don't know how to describe it; just a *weird* feeling. I'm not sure there is anybody to blame. I know we did our best, and so did you. Just can't put my finger on the why. Well, maybe next time will be better."

"What next time?" James asks.

"I mean a next time 'somewhere,' not necessarily here. I don't think I want another trip here either."

"Okay, let's all try to get a good night's sleep," Captain Hughes said. "I'm going to weigh anchor at dawn."

CHAPTER FOURTEEN

Sabotage

It is morning. True to his word, the dawn is barely breaking over the eastern horizon when Gordon comes on deck, ready to bring Siren Song to life and take her out of Lighthouse Reef. An emerging light says the sun will appear shortly, but it isn't visible yet.

Captain Hughes, now at the helm, turns the ignition key for the starboard engine, which should awaken Siren Song. But something is wrong. He doesn't hear the usual warning whistle omitted by his in-dash alarm system. He tries the port engine with the same result.

Ken is standing on the bow of the boat, waiting for the engines to roar to life so he can be ready to un-fowl the lines when they haul up the anchors. He turns and looks at Gordon, motions a 'what's up' sign and yells, "What's happening?"

"I don't know," Gordon yells back. "There's nothing. It's dead. I'm not getting power to the engines for some reason."

Ken works his way back from the bow, into the salon. "That ever happen before?"

"No. Never. This has been one of the most reliable boats I've ever known."

Gordon turns the keys off and heads for the stern. Once there, he lifts the hatch to the motor room and enters. Ken stands by in case Gordon needs anything. Gordon has turned on lights and can be heard shuffling around. Then he says, "Sonofabitch!"

"What's wrong?" Ken asks.

"Some of these cables down here managed to get shorted. Damndest thing I ever saw. Do we have any power up there at all?"

"I don't know," Ken says. He opens the door to the salon and yells in. "Hey, Angie, try the microwave or something, see if we have any power."

Angie tries the microwave. Nothing. She looks at Ken and shakes her head no.

Ken calls down to Gordon, "Hang on a second." Then Ken goes to the ship-to-shore radio and turns it on. He discovers that the radio is already turned on, but not functioning. There is apparently no power to it. Ken returns to the engine room hatch.

We don't have power to anything up here. But there must be power. You've got lights on down there."

"Those are battery powered, for just such an occasion as this," Gordon says. A moment later, Gordon appears from the engine room, motions to Ken to join him at the far stern of the boat. He speaks to Ken in hushed tones.

"There's something awful screwy going on here. I've never seen cables get that fucked up before and if I didn't know better, I would say it is intentional sabotage.

132

Somebody went down there during the night and buggered us."

"What? Who would do that?"

"I don't know. They had to know what they were doing. Those batteries are deader than a doornail. Our cell phones are worthless this far from shore. Tell you what, that Zodiac has a pull start motor on it. I'm gonna take it and go to Halfmoon Caye. It's only about seven miles from here. The lighthouse keeper has a ship to shore radio. I'm gonna call the Coast Guard and get 'em out here, pronto."

"Okay, if that's what you want to do. But if you'll just wait a while, even dead batteries will recharge themselves enough to get these engines started."

"The word 'wait' has never been in my vocabulary. By the time those batteries can build back up, I can have the Coast Guard here and we can get this damn thing going. I want to get the hell out of here before dark. You keep everybody calm. Go down into the motor room once I'm gone and see what you can do about repairing those cables. When the batteries build up enough, forget trying to start the motors, call the Coast Guard immediately. Who knows? In the meantime, maybe another boat will show up. We can always hope. Anyway, as soon as I make that call from the lighthouse keeper's radio, I'll be back."

"Good plan. Be careful going through those coral heads with that Zodiac."

"Are you kidding? That thing has a draft of about an inch!"

"Okay, good luck. I'd better get to work on those cables," Ken says, and descends the ladder into the engine room.

By now, everyone on the yacht has been roused and makes an appearance. Scott asks, "What's going on?"

Angie responds by saying, "Something entirely weird is going on. The electrical cables 'mysteriously' got messed up. Ken is going down there now to try and fix them."

Scott looks down the hatch into the engine room. "You need any help, Ken?"

"Sure. Come on." As Scott descends the ladder into the engine room, the small kicker on the back of the Zodiac comes to life. Gordon waves goodbye to everybody and begins his cautious trip through the reef to Halfmoon Caye.

Maris watches Gordon as he leaves on the Zodiac. Then she turns and feigns interest in what's going on in the engine room. After a minute or two, she yells down to Ken.

"Hey, Ken! If I'm not needed for anything, I think I'm gonna snorkel around in the shallows a little."

"Sure. Have fun," Ken says. Just be careful. I wouldn't wander too far away from the boat if I were you."

"No problem. I just want to do something...anything. It'll beat sitting around here all day."

As she walks away toward the stern gate to the dive platform, James and Angie look at one another, then shrug. "What harm can she do?" James whispers. She's taking fins, snorkel and a mask only."

"I don't know," Angie says. I just don't trust that bitch. I think everything she does is disaster, with premeditation. Besides, what does she need a scuba outfit for? She has already demonstrated that."

James hears Angie's concern, glances at Maris one last time as she goes down the ladder, says, "You've got a point." Then he turns his attention to the activity in the engine room, but suddenly has another thought.

He looks at Angie and says, "You know what we ought to do?"

"What?" she asks.

"I think this would be the perfect time to put that memory card in Gordon's laptop and see what images Scott has captured. Don't you?"

"James, that sounds like the best idea all day."

———

Maris, now a few hundred yards away from the boat, surfaces and looks back to make sure she isn't being watched. Once confirmed, she removes her mask, snorkel and swim fins, leaving them lying on the sandy bottom, under water between two coral heads. She now turns and swims at lightning speed through the coral reef toward Gordon Hughes, aboard the Zodiac.

Meanwhile, Gordon is making good time, skimming across the water in the direction of Halfmoon Caye. He is almost out of sight of Siren Song when he begins to hear a haunting woman's voice, singing. The singing is so sweet that it has the ability to rob him of his will. But something inside off him tells him he has heard this voice before, and he becomes alarmed. He takes his one hand off of the control stick and places both of his hands over his ears. He presses his hands hard against the sides of his head, trying to shut the sound of the singing out.

The sweet sound is too penetrating. It is no use. He remembers from whence this singing comes. He slows the Zodiac and lets the motor die. He looks at the bottom of the boat while he makes a final effort to rid himself of the sound. He has failed, and he knows it. He removes his hands from his head and looks up. Sure enough, Maris is sitting there, in the bow of the boat, smiling sweetly.

"Hello, Gordon," she says in a soft, seductive voice.

"It *is* you," Gordon says. "I thought so from the moment I saw you, but I couldn't be sure. You look a lot different from the last time we met. So, I decided to give you the benefit of the doubt. Stupid of me."

"Yes, I almost had you once before, didn't I? You slipped away, Gordon. You naughty boy. That wasn't nice, Gordon."

"What the hell are you talking about? You're a murderous bitch sent from hell. You've been killing men for over a thousand years. And you accuse me of being 'naughty!' I was trying to save my life, you crazy bitch."

"Yes, I know. It was quite necessary from your standpoint, I'm afraid. One must do what one must do to survive."

"Well, fuck you! I just might get away from you again."

"I don't think so, Gordon. You were younger then, and you wouldn't have made it anyway if it hadn't been for those other people."

"Why are you like this, Maris? You know, if you would try, you might find that you like people. Give them a chance and they might like you. Anybody can change if they want to."

"I didn't choose who I am, or what I am, Gordon. I just 'am'. And I'm stuck with it. It's just survival at this point. Oh, sure, I used to enjoy watching people die when I was young. But all of that got boring a long time ago. Now, I only do it for the sake of staying alive."

"Staying alive? At the expense of how many people

dying needlessly? Don't you think your time has passed? Hell, how old do you want to be?"

"I'm not human, Gordon. I'm a creature. I want to live forever. But that's getting harder to do."

"What do you mean?"

"I mean, there are more and more people coming to what you call, 'The Great Blue Hole,' just to have a good time. That was never a problem before fifty or sixty years ago. Now, every time I turn around, I have to hide from some idiot with a scuba tank and a camera. It's just a matter of time before I'm discovered and wind up on the cover of a human's fishing magazine like, 'THE SALTWATER ANGLER.' Or rather, my body will be. 'Look here, readers, catch of the week!' There is no doubt they'd kill me. I'd be a trophy on somebody's wall. People like their creatures from mythology to be in books, not real."

"That's not necessarily true."

"Don't even try, Gordon. You know as well as I do that my siren song is almost a swan song. I don't have long to go, but I have to fight for every minute of time that I can."

"You've lived too long already, Maris. You've killed, no, *murdered* too many people. How many people is that by now, Maris? Huh? How many? Don't you feel anything at all when you murder someone?"

"Relief, Gordon. Relief is what I feel. One more threat to my existence, removed."

"Let's change subject, sort of: I know you're fixing to kill me. But I've pretty well lived my life and I believe in God, which means I will go to Heaven when I die, and you certainly will not. But why not just let it end with me? Let those other people on the boat go. They're good people, and that kid hasn't even had a chance to live life yet. He's twelve years old for Christ's sake."

"Yes, well, that 'boy' is the most dangerous thing that's been thrown at me lately. Besides, he'll grow up to be a man, if I let him. Then he'll be back, and I'll have to deal with him all over again. It's better to get it over with now."

"I'm begging you, please Maris. Let them go."

"You aren't in much of a position to negotiate, Gordon. If people hear about the 'mysterious disappearance' of all aboard Siren Song at The Great Blue Hole, maybe it will keep them away... for a while at least."

"If that's what you think, you know less about humans than I thought. Something like that will have boat loads of scientists and researchers, and 'mystery solvers' out here, standing on each other's shoulders, checking every square inch of this place. It'll be on the cover of every magazine known to man."

"I'll have to take that chance. Come on, Gordon. We need to get on with this."

Gordon looks at her, measures her, wonders if he can take her. "I'm tired anyway. Just try to be as gentle as you can."

"You won't feel a thing. You can even have me before I 'have' you if you would like."

"What? I don't know about that Maris. You aren't even a real woman."

"Give it a try. You might find that I'm the most 'woman' thing you've ever had. Why, you might even die with a smile on your lips."

"I seriously doubt that. Make love to a vicious, rapacious, murdering bitch like you? I don't think so. But I do have just one last question. Did you kill D J?"

"He would have had to go sooner or later anyway. He just found out about me at the wrong time. Sorry. It was necessary."

"Dammit. He was a good kid. Dammit again! He... oh man, I hate that. That hurts my heart." Bending over in his pain, through his tears, Gordon sees an oyster knife lying in the bottom of the Zodiac, wedged against the inflated edge off the craft. As he falls down on his knees, pretending to cry, he reaches down with his right hand and palms the oyster knife.

"Are you ready now, Gordon?" he hears Maris say.

"As ready as I'll ever be. How are you going to do it? What do you want me to do to make it easier on me?"

"Make love to me, Gordon. In the sea. It's so much sweeter there."

Without a word, Gordon obediently slips over the side of the Zodiac into the water. Maris is suddenly there beside him and starts undressing him, then herself. She smiles at him. Wraps her arms around his neck and begins kissing him. He returns her passionate kiss, while at the same time wrapping his arms around her. Then, with all the strength he can muster, he plunges the oyster knife into her back. She opens her mouth wide and gasps in pain. Desperately, Maris struggles to reach behind her and pull the knife out, but she cannot reach it.

While she struggles and writhes in the water, she momentarily releases her hold on Gordon, who takes advantage of the moment to push her away.

"That's for D J, you murdering cunt from hell!"

Then, Gordon scrambles back into the Zodiac. Frantically, he yanks on the pull rope, once, then twice. The small motor doesn't start. If it fails a third time, he is dead.

He quickly makes an adjustment on the control stick and yanks again. The motor hums to life. Yelling "FUCK YOU!" over the side of the boat, he revs the motor and speeds away from Maris, pointing the Zodiac toward Halfmoon Caye.

Meanwhile, Maris gasps and struggles with her wound. Gordon has done well—Maris is badly wounded. But is she dying? She hopes not. The possibility makes her more determined than ever to dispatch the rest of the people aboard Siren Song.

———

Aboard Siren Song, Ken looks out at the coral surrounding the boat. He's starting to look worried.

"Maris is overdue. I don't see her anywhere. I'm going out there to look for her."

James and Angie look at one another. Then, after a minute of deliberation, they approach Ken who is gathering his fins and mask.

"Uh, Ken. I know this is going to sound crazy, but we wish you wouldn't do that," Angie says, hesitantly.

Ken's brow wrinkles as he turns to look at Angie. "She might be in trouble out there somewhere. I don't understand what you're saying."

"Yeah, I know you don't. Ahh, Ken, James and I have something we need to tell you."

Angie takes Ken by the hand and pulls him toward the sofa. "Come over here and sit down a minute. I don't really know how to say this because you are going to think James and I are suffering from nitrogen narcosis, or worse. You'll think we're completely bananas."

"What are you talking about?" Ken asks as he sinks down onto the sofa. Angie stands in front of him, beside James.

"Ken, we believe that Maris is...a creature from mythology."

"What?"

"A siren, or at least, a mutation, a hybrid of a siren."

"Some kind of a specie of a siren," James adds, nodding his head yes.

To Angie's surprise, Ken sits watching her, completely silent.

"There isn't time to explain all of it, but there has been some pretty screwball things happen on this trip, not the least of which is the disappearance of D J. And now, the boat being disabled here in the middle of the Blue Hole. Scott took some pictures the other day and one or more of them might show something. Maris stole the memory card out of Scott's camera and buried it in a shallow hole. Luckily, James saw her do it and retrieved the card. We've been trying to get the card in that lap-top in there, but we need an adaptor. The minute we fit it in, no telling what we'll see."

Ken takes a deep breath. "I don't know what to say. I'm sure you must know how over the top all this sounds. If I didn't know both of you, and feel that you are level-headed people... Still, if you're wrong, and I think you probably are, that girl could be in trouble out there. I have a responsibility not only as dive master, but as a representative of Sport Divers of Houston Tours. We're the ones that offered this trip, charged money for it. The safety of all passengers aboard rests on my shoulders. Now, if I wait for you to find an adaptor, which you may or may not do... I can just see myself trying to explain to some judge why I didn't go looking for one of my charges. 'I thought she was a siren, your honor, and didn't need me.' Wonder how many years I'd get when the judge stopped laughing?"

Angie got in front of Ken, who was now rising from the sofa. "If we're right, and if you do go out there, she could be waiting for you right this minute! She might be out there, watching this boat, baiting you, not coming back here on purpose, knowing you will come looking for her."

"So? What is it you think she will do?"

"We think she will *kill you*. We think she wants to kill everyone on this boat."

"You're kidding!"

"No, I wish we were. We aren't."

"Well, it's just a chance I'm going to have to take. First, the human aspect. Next, I don't want to get sued for negligence." Ken walks to the stern of the boat, closely followed by James and Angie.

"I don't think you're hearing us. She will kill you," Angie pleads. If we all stay together, we might stand a chance. She's frightened of James."

By now, Angie is shouting and near hysteria. Ken starts putting on his scuba gear, preparing for an underwater search. He tries to ignore Angie and James, not wanting to so much as think about her last remark, much less give it credence. When he goes off of the dive platform into the water, Angie turns quickly and says to James, "Let's figure out some way to get that damned memory card in the laptop."

The two of them disappear into the salon.

Scott watches them. Then, when they are out of sight, he

turns to Al, who has been in a lounge chair on the stern the whole time, listening to the frantic exchange.

Scott asks, "Do you know what the hell they're talking about?"

Al nods his head. "Yeah, I'm afraid I do. You better have a seat. This is gonna take some time to explain."

Meanwhile, Ken Malloy has barely gotten in the water and cleared his mask when he feels somebody tap him on the shoulder. He spins around in the water and is surprised to see Maris there. Not only does she have no dive gear on, she is completely nude. She has no tank, no fins, no mask, nothing.

Ken Malloy's eyes grow big as something unhuman in appearance, something like a tentacle comes at him and wraps around his neck.

In the boat, Al Harmon is in the middle of explaining what is going on to Scott. If either of them had been looking anywhere besides at each other, if they would have been looking at the water anywhere around the boat, they would have seen that water turn bright red with a huge, expanding cloud of blood.

In the salon, Angie gets frustrated, trying everything she can think of to fit the memory card into the laptop computer.

"Wait a minute!" James says. "We're going about this all wrong."

"What are you talking about?" Angie asks, as she fusses with the computer.

"All we have to do is put the card back into Scott's camera and turn it on. Doesn't his camera have a read-out window to check his shots? I think most cameras do."

"Angie blinks. "James, you're right. Let me go get Scott's camera."

Meanwhile, Al Harmon has been constantly taking pain medicine on top of J D, and for all intents, is out of it. Having finished his explanation to Scott, he lolls on the lounge chair, half zonked.

Scott decides to go into the salon and see what Angie and James are up to. But just before he slides the door open, he hears singing so sweet that it is as if it is from an angel. He is captivated and must go where he can be closer to the source. Scott forgets about going into the salon. Instead, he turns and goes to where the scuba gear sits at the ready. He slips on a geared-up BC, grabs mask and fins and makes his way toward the ladder at the back of the boat.

Angie has retrieved Scott's camera. Quickly, she and James scan the dozens of pictures taken by Scott. Then, they find what they are looking for. Angie squints as she focuses on the small picture.

"Ohhhhhh my God!" she says in horror. "That's what she looks like when she's not in drag?"

"So it would seem," James says. "Well, there's no doubt anymore. Not that there really was any doubt by now. This is proof. Confirmation of everything we have suspected all along. And now that we know that for sure, we know the rest is for sure. She has to kill us all. She thinks it's the only way she can survive."

Just at that moment, they hear a splash that is the sound of Scott going overboard.

"Oh, shit! What was that?" Angie asks.

"It can't be good," James says. Both of them rush outside the salon and look around, then James looks over the side and down. Sure enough, he sees Scott going straight down into the Blue Hole. Scott may be hypnotized. Maris is close at his side, with her arm around him. She is completely nude, but bleeding from her back close to the left shoulder blade.

"Maris has Scott. She's gonna kill him," James says, then he turns and quickly starts gearing up. "Go get the bang stick, Angie," James says.

Angie turns and moves like a rabbit into her state-room where she has kept James' bang stick. She also grabs a couple of .357 bullets and loads the head of the stick. She returns very quickly with the sick and hands it to James, as well as the extra bullet.

"Wish me luck," James says, and unceremoniously falls backwards off the gunwale of Siren Song, rolls over in the water and heads straight down as fast as he can swim.

Al Harmon, who is still half out of it, struggles up from his chair, staggers toward Angie, who is peering over the side, and says, "What's going on?"

"Maris has Scott," Angie says. "James has gone after them."

"Maris?"

"She really is a siren, Al. She wants to kill us all. Everybody."

"Good God! Then it's true."

"Very true. And now she is pulling Scott down into the hole to kill him."

"Did you say James has gone after them?"

"Yes. He's down there now. They've already passed through the thermocline. James is almost there." Angie's voice quavers as she wipes away tears that keep clouding her vision.

Al looks up. "Great-great-Grampa, if you're up there watching this, please protect our boy."

Meanwhile, James, closing in on the thermocline, has

one hand on his nose so he can equalize and the other hand on the bang stick. This is no slow, comfortable descent. James pushes with his fins and legs as hard as he can to close in on Maris and Scott.

He goes through the thermocline like an arrow. The grottos are clearly visible below. So far, Maris is unaware that James is behind them, closing in. She swims casually with her intended victim. It appears her intention is to take Scott into the grottos. What she plans to do there, her method of dispatching Scott, only she knows.

As James comes eye level with the grottos, he immediately spots Maris and Scott. They are on the floor of the grotto, adjacent to a fallen stalactite. Maris has already removed Scott's mask and regulator. She has her arms and legs wrapped around him. She is vamping him, even as she plasters her lips against his and sucks his breath out of him.

James hurls his body toward them in a fantastic burst of energy and speed. It is as though a special force is assisting him. He is moving so fast when he reaches them that he cannot stop and crashes into them with the power of a piledriver, which causes Maris to lose her grip on Scott. The siren is totally taken by surprise. James' appearance and attack on her has broken her concentration, and thus her spell on Scott is also dissolved.

Scott reaches frantically for his regulator and mask. But now, Maris turns her wrath upon James. Instinctively, she knows this little prepubescent bastard is her worst nightmare. If he has not grown close enough to manhood, she has no power over him, so she must resort to something else. She tries her hypnotic song anyway, but it is having no effect on him, and he is now taking the bang stick in both hands as he swims toward her.

Relying on her ability to morph, she transforms her appearance quickly. She changes into her true self, a grotesque sea monster. The ugliness is incredible, repulsive enough to make a person's gorge rise. It causes James to pause for what could be a life altering, deadly moment, so that he can avert his eyes. This is what Maris was hoping for. She moves toward James.

A horrible looking tentacle reaches out and tries to take the bang stick away from James. The tentacle wraps around the bang-stick and begins pulling with amazing strength. She almost has it, but James regroups. He realizes how close to death he is. And if he dies, then so will everyone aboard Siren Song.

He yanks back hard, taking the weapon away from this horrid monster confronting him. Then he lunges forward, bang stick protruding and pointed directly at the monster. He musters every ounce of determination in himself.

At this very moment, he feels other, larger, more powerful hands than his, helping him. The hands are being placed on top of his, assisting him with extra strength. James is being visited by his great–great grandfather. The family ancestor has been guiding James the whole time, after all.

The bang stick connects with the siren's lower chest and James pushes hard. There is a sickening 'thump-like' explosion as the weapon discharges.

Maris grabs at her chest and bends over in pain. Her eyes are wide open with shock. She opens her mouth and there is an agonized sound that comes out, a scream, inhuman, but loud, penetrating.

Spreading blood oozes from Maris' wound and clouds the water around her. When James squints to see through the cloud of blood, Maris has changed back into a beautiful woman. She holds her midriff but looks at James with pleading eyes as if it was she who was betrayed, and perhaps she was. Not by the humans she intended to kill, but by her birth-right.

James removes the regulator from his mouth long enough to say, "Goodbye, Maris," Then he replaces the regulator in his mouth, fits the second bullet into the bang stick and charges the monster again. A second explosion is heard. Maris again shrieks in pain.

James removes his regulator once again. "Did that hurt?" he says sarcastically. The words came out obscured by copious exhaled bubbles, but that's okay. James feels sure she understood anyway. After all, she's a fucking sea monster, right?

Two more times Maris changes from a woman into a monster and back again, as she grows weaker and weaker. In her dying moments, Maris manages a weak smile at James, and reaches out to him and tries her siren coo, even as she slowly sinks toward the bottom of The Great Blue Hole.

James suddenly feels himself responding to the sound of her voice and must turn away quickly, or he will be compelled to go to her rescue. His boyhood is quickly fading, replaced by manhood.

But for now, as Maris sinks slowly out of sight, James goes to where Scott is clinging to one of the stalactites. The man is suffering from mild shock, but James manages to get a grip on his shoulders and shakes him back into reality. When James gets a nod of okay from Scott, they exit the grotto and begin their trip to the surface, one hundred and fifty feet above.

———

It is late afternoon aboard Siren Song. Scott Carrington is now the one spread out on the large sofa in the salon. Angie tenderly attends to him, applying cool cloths to his forehead.

Captain Gordon Hughes stands in the stern area of Siren Song, staring at nothing in particular.

In the salon, at the console, Al Harmon reaches for the ship to shore radio, James stands next to him. James crosses his fingers. "You think the batteries are recovered enough?"

"Dey recovahed!" Chester says.

"We're about to find out," his father says.

He turns the radio on. A moment later, there is static. Al presses the talk button on the microphone. "This is the pleasure craft Siren Song calling Belize Coast Guard. Do you read? Over."

There is several seconds of silence. Al is about to try again when suddenly, "This is Belize Coast Guard. We read you loud and clear, Siren Song." The voice has a distinct Belizian accent.

Al speaks again. "Mayday, Mayday. This is a distress call. We are at The Great Blue Hole and we are disabled. We need assistance. Over."

"Yes, we have been advised," the coast guard voice said. "Mister Michael from Robert's Grove Resort called several hours ago. He said he hadn't heard from you and was worried. We have a cutter en route as well as a chopper. One or the other should be there in a few minutes. Can you last that long? Over."

"Ha! That is excellent news. We can last. We aren't sinking, just disabled. Over."

"Are there any injuries? Over."

"Affirmative. Two missing, one on board is in shock, and one with a dislocated shoulder. Over."

The voice sounded a little more concerned this time. "I understand. I will notify the cutter. They will get there as fast as they can and organize a search. Over and out."

"Thank you. Siren Song, out," Al said, and laid down the microphone. Then he says to James, "Understand? He could never 'understand'. I'm not sure that I understand. All I know is, I am thankful to Great-great-Grampa. I believe in my heart he was there with you today."

"No doubt!" James says.

As the sun sinks closer to the horizon, we see Siren Song from the very center of the surface of the Great Blue Hole. The water is flat, not a ripple. You can hear various voices coming from the boat. They are happy voices because the Belize Coast Guard is about to arrive and lend assistance. All is calm.

And then, something slowly rises from the depths. It's hard to tell what it is. It looks like a head wearing a crown of feathers, but that can't be right. Whatever it is, it stares without moving, in the direction of Siren Song.

The End

———

Don't miss out on your next favorite book!
Join the Melange Books mailing list at
www.melange-books.com/mail.html

THANK YOU FOR READING

———

Did you enjoy this book?

We invite you to leave a review at your favorite book site, such as Goodreads, Amazon, Barnes & Noble, etc.

DID YOU KNOW THAT LEAVING A REVIEW...

- Helps other readers find books they may enjoy.
- Gives you a chance to let your voice be heard.
- Gives authors recognition for their hard work.
- Doesn't have to be long. A sentence or two about why you liked the book will do.

 **GEORGE DISMUKES** spent the first half of his life in pursuit of adventure. This ranged from bullfighting as a youth to milking poisonous snakes professionally at Ross Allen's Reptile Institute in Silver Springs, Florida. The early 60s found him pursuing wild animals across the Serengeti in the movie business and operating an animal export company in Iquitos, Peru. He spent many years exploring archaeological sites of the ancient Maya Indians in Central America and studying their lost civilization. He also lived in Honduras, where the story, TWO FACES OF THE JAGUAR, THE LOST CITY, and THE JAGUAR'S QUEST take place.

In 1980, he began a video production company in Houston, Texas and worked as a 'triple threat' (writer/director/producer) creating some of the Houston market's most creative television commercials. He won a CLEO award for his production of a series of television PSAs concerning prevention of child abuse, funded through a grant from the University of Houston.

Currently, he lives on the Texas Coast with his soul mate and closest friend, Nadine, where he writes and works in magazine advertising. His hobbies include growing exotic chili peppers and experimenting with salsa recipes. Above all, George is a devout animal lover and advocate, fighting against animal abuse. He has two dogs, named Pulga and Gizmo, respectively.

twitter.com/@dismukesgeorge

ALSO BY GEORGE DISMUKES

Two Faces of the Jaguar

The Lost City

Jaguar's Quest